tales of the
BAGMAN
VOLUME III

AIRSHIP 27 PRODUCTIONS

Tales of the Bagman Volume 3
© 2016 B.C. Bell

Published by Airship 27 Productions
www.airship27.com
www.airship27hangar.com

Interior illustrations © 2016 Art Cooper
Cover illustration © 2016 Shane Evans

Editor: Ron Fortier
Associate Editor:Fred Adams Jr.
Marketing and Promotions Manager: Michael Vance
Production and design by Rob Davis.

ISBN-13: 978-0692636305 (Airship 27)
ISBN-10: 0692636307

Printed in the United States of America

10 9 8 7 6 5 4 3 2 1

tales of the BAGMAN
VOLUME III

TABLE OF CONTENTS

THE BUTCHER
BACK O' THE YARDS
by B. C. Bell

The south side of Chicago wasn't the baddest part of town. In fact, the Bridgeport neighborhood of Mayor Ed Kelley was also home to some of the most exclusive real estate in the city. Set well back from the main thoroughfares, ballparks and bars, Kelley's subdivision seemed to be an elite section of the city all its own. A small block of gated homes with half-acre yards, looping driveways, gothic columns and marble stairs.

Nobody asked how a public employee could afford such a mansion. But Kelley had run for mayor on the platform of *not* being a reformer, which had made him the perfect politcian for Chicago during Prohibition. He was expected to take a few liberties with the city's illegal business as usual. So he did. Given that the city's previous mayor, Anton Cermak, had been assassinated, not too many people held the graft against Mayor Ed. Very few, in fact.

Unfortunately for Kelley, one of the few was a man from the north side.

"You guys can take the rest of the night off," Kelley said, entering the luxurious estate's entry hall. "I've got some paperwork to go over before morning, and I won't need anything till breakfast."

"You want me to stay in the servant's quarters in case the family needs anything?" the chauffeur asked.

"Nah, family's all gone to visit Grandma, so for once I can get a little work done. Just make sure you're here early in the morning."

"In that case, I got a gentleman's club to visit, see a man about a dog," the third man in the lobby, most likely a bodyguard said. "See ya in the funny papers."

"Early," Kelley reminded him.

"I'll be in the servant's quarters," the chauffeur said. "By the time I had enough to drink, it'd be daylight already anyway." The servant's quarters were located in a coach house half an acre away.

The man from the north side stood in the shadows, unseen, unknown, and smiled to himself.

Mayor Kelly locked the door behind him and turned to face a gigantic entryway with marble steps running up each side of the walls. He smiled to himself, glanced at the bedroom on the left hand side, then headed up the steps to the office on the right. Pulling a key out of his pocket, he unlocked the door and switched the den lights on before turning the hall light off.

It was a large room with vaulted ceilings and bookcases built into two walls. Three wooden file cabinets and an oak wardrobe stood on one wall, across from and beneath an array of plaques and pictures declaring Ed Kelley a friend of the community and the world at large. All this stood only to draw one's attention to an oak desk the size of a garage door standing just inside the shaded picture windows in back.

With a gleam in his eye, Kelley pulled the key back out of his pocket and unlocked the antique cabinet by the wall, revealing it to be a secret wet bar. The Mayor poured himself a tumbler of rye, swirled it around in the glass and took a sip. Humming tunelessly to himself, he poured some more and, contemplating the amber liquid, circled the room toward his desk.

He was almost dancing as he pulled the chain attached to the banker's lamp, and a green glow illuminated the rest of room. He was about to sit down, when he glanced up and his whole body hitched like he'd been hit with a jolt of electricity. The glass tumbler fell from his hand, bounced off the Persian rug and rolled back-and-forth across the hardwood.

Kelley gasped. Then there was a moment of deadly silence. You could almost hear the liquor run through the floorboards.

Mayor Ed bordered on panic because the desk lamp had illuminated a lot more than the scattered City of Chicago forms normally kept on top of his desk. No, this time, that banker's lamp had lit up all the illegal books he normally kept locked inside the wall safe. And, behind those stacks of red and black binders, legal and cooked books, there had been a man. A masked man.

Not your ordinary masked man at that.

He didn't sport the stylish domino mask of a gentleman bandit of the day. Neither did he opt for the handkerchief pulled over the bottom half of his face like the usual Chicago armed robber. Instead, he wore what looked like a burlap bag over his head. It was both uncomfortable looking and strange. Like some kind of Western vigilante, except the fedora wedged over the mask was thoroughly modern. Two blue-gray eyes burned from beneath the hat's snap brim. And for a moment, without even realizing it, Mayor Ed Kelley questioned the nature of evil.

The eyes looked angry, but you could tell the man was smiling beneath the mask, like a cat with a mouse. It was a scary combination.

"Spilled your drink, Ed." The masked man stood up and waved his arm inviting Kelley to take a seat. Then he bent over, picked up Kelley's glass and sniffed the inside of it. "Rye, huh. I think you're going to need some more."

"How—how did *you* get in here?" Kelley still stood in front of the desk, gasping. "You're him, aren't you—that, that Bagman."

The Bagman wasn't just Chicago's latest mystery man, he was a complete mystery. Appearing six weeks ago, the Criminal Detective had suddenly burst on the scene holding Chicago's 42nd Precinct at bay with a hand grenade, then taking down an entire branch of the Chicago Outfit the next week. Since then, he'd taken out a gang of crooked cops and saved the World's Fair from a terrorist. He was wanted by both sides of the law, liked by neither. The only thing anybody knew about him was that he was dangerous.

"I kind of like '*The*' Bagman better." He motioned, spelling out a billboard with his hand. "Separates me from the rest of the rabble, if you know what I mean." The masked man walked over to the disguised wet bar, popped it with the heel of his leather-clad palm and opened the door. "Sit down, Ed. Get out a pencil and some paper. I'll get you a drink."

"H-how did you get in here?" the Mayor rattled.

"Puh-lease, you think I'm going to miss a chance to explore a sliding bookcase?"

Kelly sat down. The Bagman filled a tumbler halfway with Rye.

"You can press that little alarm button under your desk all you want to," The Bagman said. "It's disconnected. Again, you think I'm going to miss a chance to—"

Staring at the big man's back the entire time, Kelly's shaking right hand drifted gradually toward the top desk drawer, as if it were testing the temperature of the air.

"Don't worry about the gun, either. I already took it out of there." The Bagman turned with a drink in one hand and a small pistol spinning in the other. ".22—man I hate these things. Seriously, got just enough power to punch a hole in you, and then just bounce around in your gut." He slammed the tumbler on the table. "Have a drink, Ed."

Mayor Kelly slugged down half the glass of liquor. His tumbler rattled as his still-shaking hand placed it back on the desk.

"Are you going to kill me?" The Mayor stared at his glass, unable to look at the masked man.

"Oh, p'shaw and piffle, Mayor. 'I come not to bury Caesar but to praise him.'"

The Mayor's form visibly sunk in the chair at the Shakespearean quote. It was the same thing Brutus had said right before he'd stabbed Caesar.

"No, I'm not going to kill you—unless you make me. This is politics Ed, plain and simple, we just have to talk. See, it's about this Bagman Task Force you set up with the police. Now, I know you have to cover your ass with Frank Nitti's mob, but every cop in the city already wants to take a shot at me, and you're just making it worse. Personally, I think the city funds could be put to better use. And I think you're just the guy to find that use."

"I can't surrender the city to a masked man."

"Get out your pencil and paper."

Mayor Ed reached for the thin middle drawer this time. He put the paper and pencil on the desk before picking the pencil back up.

"I want you to write this down, Ed," the masked man said, stepping back in the bar's direction. "I, Mayor Ed Kelly, being of corrupt mind and poor mental hygiene, hereby pledge to call off the Chicago Police Department's Bagman Task Force."

The Mayor huffed and shifted in seat like he was chafing, pretending to write. He stopped, finished off his drink. The Bagman whirled, slammed another highball on the desk instantly. The mayor flinched.

"Drink up," the masked man said. "And keep writing. I need you to remember this later." Completely ignoring Mayor Kelly, the Bagman turned his back to him, and strolled back and forth in front of the bar.

"Let's see now, where was I? Oh, yeah, 'Should I welch on this deal and continue to harass the north side's handsomest masked hero ever, I will come home to find every slot machine I hold an interest in removed from 'said north side' and placed directly on my front lawn—along with all the other rigged gambling paraphernalia and half the city's unemployed musicians.'" He turned back around with another drink in his hand. "Not to mention all the minor city problems that can be avoided by not going to war with our own. And, forthwith, *our own*, also meaning, and as in, all the relatives, cronies and cutbacks in these cute little red books you got here."

"Those books have nothing to do with city business," the Mayor accidentally confessed.

"And that's my case, your not-so-honorable, quid pro crow," the Bagman announced, extending both arms in the air, and nodding his head as if to say I-told-you-so. "Habeus corpus, delectables and all."

"You're never going to get out of here alive." Kelly's hand shook holding the pen. He put it down and picked up his drink.

"The trick is not to care," the Bagman said.

It made Kelly cringe. The guy not only got on your nerves, but he knew every annoying way in the world to do it. His voice was scary one minute, sarcastic and funny the next. He talked when you didn't want him to, and shut up when you wanted him to talk. He never stayed on subject, never answered questions, and only left you with more.

Kelly gulped down his drink. The Bagman slammed another double of rye on the desk.

"Hope you took copious notes 'cause if you forget this stuff, I'm going to have to come back and beat you up." The Bagman sat on the edge of the desk, picked up Kelly's notes and rifled through them.

Kelly clinched his fists. There it was again. Being irritating, just to be irritating! 'Beat you up'? What kind of mobster says *I'm going to 'beat you up.'* Men were supposed to say they were going to kill you, rub you out, whack you, bury you, murder you, and grind you into dust. Not *'beat you up.'* It was the kind of thing school kids said. He wanted to strangle this character.

"So, drink up," the masked man said, jotting a few lines down on Kelly's notes.

"You trying to get me drunk, huh?" Kelly gulped half the glass down.

"Judging from your notes, I'm already a little late for that. No, what I'm going to do is walk out the front door and across the property. You and I both know, tonight, there's nobody here to stop me."

"It's going to take a lot more than a few drinks to knock me out, yah amateur."

"Yeah, that's why I drugged your liquor. Sorry about that, but I got to say, for a guy with money you got lousy taste in booze. I think *me* forcing *you* to restock your illegal bar could turn out to be a very good thing for you in the long run."

Kelly jumped to his feet and fell over the desk swinging at the stranger.

The Bagman laughed. It was loud, raucous and intimidating. He was cracking himself up and, once again, irritating the hell out of Mayor Ed Kelly.

Kelly's limbs flailed across the top of the desk, his body flopping like a beached sea animal as he tried to regain his footing. The Bagman grabbed him by the hair, and slapped him across the face, backhanding him twice.

"Don't make me kill you, Ed. I'd like it too much." He wrapped his fingers around Kelly's face and shoved him back into his seat. Picking the tumbler up off the table, he slammed it on the desk in front of the Mayor.

"Drink." The Man of Steal leaned over, his fists on the desk.

Mayor Ed Kelly's eyes were the size of saucers.

Staring down at him was no normal man. He was like a force. A man who didn't operate by the channels Ed Kelly was used to. Hell, the channels anybody was used to. And for a man who made his living figuring people out like the Mayor did, that was frightening. His chest felt tight. He picked up the glass and gulped part of it down.

The Bagman patted him on the back.

"So it's simple, really, Ed. We just keep things the way they are, only without the Task Force. It's a no-brainer."

Mayor Kelly threw up across the top of his desk. His head reeled in the air a moment, before he landed face down on it. He made a spluttering sound, then another, then he started snoring between the spluttering.

The Bagman approached from where he'd jumped to avoid the Mayor's cookies.

"I was going to say it was a cream puff, but I figured a no-brainer would be lot easier for a guy like you to understand."

He picked up Kelly's head, turned it sideways so the Mayor could breathe and put the papers he'd been holding where Kelly would find them in the morning. Grabbing one of the red books off the table, he switched off the lights and made his way out.

The next day, the chauffeur in the stable house would remember an insane, guttural cackle on the street, the stuff of men in straitjackets whose laughter echoed more like questions than statements.

It didn't look like Mayor Ed was going to be making that morning meeting after all.

•••

Peeling his mask off before opening the door, the Mayor's visitor strolled leisurely across the lawn, combing his copper-brown hair down with one hand before putting his fedora back on at just the right angle. As if acknowledging an old friend, he half-smiled at the moon over his shoulder and drifted back east toward the railroad tracks.

The young man's name was Frank "Mac" McCullough, and, while you may have been able to see his face, he was as much a mystery as his alter ego. After the death of his father, McCullough had taken to the road as a child, where he'd learned to survive working as a thief, con-man, and hired muscle. Six weeks ago he'd returned to the city and found some work as a bagman for the mob, collecting for a loan shark. The problem was they had wanted him to collect from his Uncle Ray.

Instead of breaking Uncle Ray's legs, Mac broke his partner's nose. Then he found out, he'd been working for the same man who had killed his father. Forced to disguise himself, Mac had seized a grocery bag, put it over his head, and somehow managed to fight the mob and the police to a stand-off. The newspapers had dubbed him the Bagman.

Mac had been through a series of masks since then, but the current "burlap bag" was his favorite. It had been given to him two weeks ago by a Gypsy Fortuneteller who had told him he was the King of Thieves. Not that he necessarily believed the legend, but he really liked "the bag." It was scary looking—and silk lined.

Never one to ignore impulse, the young man decided to hop a trolley back to the Loop and see what was going on there, before taking the train back to the north side. He walked briskly down the street, his footsteps a pulse beat. Some of the tough guys in the alleys turned away when he stepped in and out of the shadows. Others waved hello.

Making his way to a speakeasy off Grand Avenue, almost across the street from the Tribune, Mac stepped inside with no questions asked. He was greeted in a backroom by a Mr. Quirt and several others. Quirt, who displayed scars on both sides of his mouth, as if someone had tried to cut it open even wider, mentioned a fur robbery. The big man said he'd be interested, talked about baseball for a while and then left, hustling for the Ravenswood El and home.

He was feeling pretty satisfied with himself. It had been a good night's work, and now that he'd set up plans for a fur robbery, he'd have even more work. Because Mac was the guy who stole from the bad guys.

Given Mac's criminal background it was no surprise that the Bagman was no enforcer of the law, but rather a protector of those that fell between the cracks, and a destroyer of men who took advantage of them. Justice was a pretty broad and bandied about term in 1933 Chicago and, much like Mayor Ed Kelly, the fact that it was ill-defined at best worked to the Bagman's advantage. The Bagman stole justice because to him that made sense. Not much else in his world did.

●●●

"Ethics change, morality doesn't."

"What's that even mean, Mac?" the bartender said. He didn't know Mac's name, he was just one of those guys that called everybody Mac.

"It means the goals are still the same, but how you go about getting 'em is different."

"So you think it's OK? A guy like Cobb sharpening his spikes, bunting and trying to take out the first baseman?"

"See, Cobb's baseball ethics outweigh his morality. He has to win. It isn't nice, but c'mon!" Mac pointed at the bartender as if he'd made a point, then waved the thought away with one motion of his hand. "Bad enough they ruled out the spitball! Rule out intimidating the other guy, and the next thing you know the batters will all be wearing helmets!" He sat back in his chair, scoffing.

It was the next afternoon, and justice, ethics and morality being what they were, Mac McCullough had stopped into his favorite neighborhood speakeasy to listen to a ballgame on the radio while killing time before meeting a friend on the other side of the Ravenswood tracks.

Barney's Grill deserved to be called a blind pig more than a speakeasy. Not the nicest place, but still the one Mac frequented the most. These days it almost resembled a real barroom, and the fact that it wasn't raided daily was a definite sign that Prohibition was on its last legs. Originally named Barney's *Bar and* Grill, the sign out front had a two foot gap between the words "Barney's" and "Grill," where somebody had slapped some paint over the words "Bar and." Nobody knew who Barney was.

"Still, somebody spikes me bad, I'm going to be clobbering 'em after the game," Mac said. "That's just not good business with what goes around coming around, y'know? I always liked coming in low, bowling 'em over, anyhow."

"You would. Look at ya, Mac. No offense, but you're built like a gorilla."

Mac gave him a stern look.

"I mean like Honus Wagner. Some of these other guys ain't got your built in skills, see. It's a sucker bet."

"Skills?" Mac McCullough laughed. "I run a cigar store." Mac owned Mac's Tobacco on Lincoln Avenue down the street. He'd bought the store planning to retire from crime, but soon it had become a respectable front for the rest of Mac's not-so respectable undertakings.

"Looks like a real tough job," the bartender said, toweling off the bar. "How's business over there?"

"Lousy, that's why I got somebody watching the store for me." Mac stared at his beer. "I'm looking for prospects."

The bartender was inspecting Mac's drink for potential prospects when a loud thump shook the floor beneath them, which wasn't entirely surprising. Being a second floor speakeasy, it was common for somebody who'd already had a few to get eighty-sixed on the stairway below. Barney's was set up to be a one-story establishment, with the grill on the first floor as a legitimate front. The grill man downstairs was actually a bouncer named Popeye, the kind of guy that spent his nights off shooting dice and picking fights on the docks, thus the nickname. If you were lucky, he might be able to cook you a hamburger.

Mac's bartender opened his mouth again to say something, but stopped when he heard the rumble of a truck in the "abandoned garage" below, where the beer kegs and a stock of liquor were stored. Nobody was supposed to be down there except for deliveries. Nobody.

He stood at attention. There was a crash and a man screamed downstairs. A gun fired and the bullet penetrated the floor just to Mac's left. He could see the hole in the floor where it had just missed his foot. The bartender grabbed a sawed-off shotgun from behind the bar, and made his way toward the staircase door.

•••

"Stay here."

A hand like a monkey wrench grabbed him by the shoulder. The bartender stopped and turned. Mac pulled a snub nose revolver out his holster, let go of the man and thumbed over his shoulder behind the bar, toward the sliding panel in the wall that was supposed to be a secret exit.

"Why don't you lead the rest of the crowd outside, see what's going on below? I'll go down front."

The bartender eyed Mac for a moment. Then the gun.

"You're right. Just take it easy with the gat, OK? It's bad for business." The bartender waved his hand and started to signal for an evacuation, but the other three people in the room were already lined up behind the bar. He shrugged at Mac and opened the door in the paneling.

Mac nodded and headed for the front. Downstairs, he twisted the lock, stepped back, and kicked the door open.

So much for the element of surprise. Mac stood looking at the inside of the barrels of two .45 automatics. The men holding them were young and dressed sharp, tailored three-piece suits and silver plated guns. To McCullough's left a bruiser in a dented derby and overalls gripped the struggling grill man in a headlock. The aggressor looked more like a farmer than a mobster. Mac could see the burns on the Popeye's face where they'd held it against the grill. The man holding him still had a sap in one of his hands.

Mac dropped his gun.

"What seems to be the problem here?" he asked in a deceptively civil tone.

"No problem, Buddy, no problem. Just delivering some beer," the smaller man who seemed to be in charge said. He leveled his gun at Mac.

"We didn't order no beer," Popeye grumbled, still trying to shrug off the headlock.

"Well, you should'a because that swill you've been serving is running all your customers off."

"I don't need no beer," Popeye said.

"Sure you do. Our sales consultant checked your stock and it's desperately low," the smaller man said.

That very second, somebody opened the door to the back warehouse where the beer was stored. A crew of two men unloaded kegs from a truck in back, while another held the bartender and another employee from upstairs at gunpoint. Beer was all over the floor of the back garage, Mac could smell it waft in. The men had broken all the old kegs in the back.

"So, I guess we do need some beer," Mac said. He smiled his best corn-fed rube smile.

Popeye wanted to kill somebody. "We don't need no—"

The man with the sap knocked him out. Popeye slid out of his arms to the floor. Their guns were all pointed at Mac now.

"You the owner here?" the leader of the gang said.

"No, just a guy who likes beer," Mac said, holding his hands in the air. "And not trouble."

The smaller gangster smiled at him as if Mac were weak and shoved him toward the back room. "Well, tell the owner it looks like you're going to need another delivery," he said, locking Mac up with the staff in the garage. "We'll send another shipment in a couple days!"

The captives could hear the bootleggers laughing through the door.

"Everybody OK here?" Mac said.

The men in line nodded, while still turning their heads over all the spilt beer. Mac made his way to the back and checked the lock on the garage door. They'd broken it and probably bolted the door outside somehow, too. The big man grabbed a hammer and screwdriver off a work bench, waded through the suds to the grill room and began knocking the front door off its hinges. In less than three minutes they were free.

●●●

Ignoring the rest of the crowd, Mac sprinted for the street. A red Pierce Arrow screeched its tires as it took the corner a block away. He couldn't read the license plate. He could always just wait for the men to come back with the next delivery, but he didn't want to wait that long. And there on the corner just behind him—like a message from God—stood a two-tone Marmon 16 Victoria Club. Mac remembered his mechanic buddy, Crankshaft, saying Marmon was a genius. Sixteen cylinders and top of the line, it was a really nice car.

So nice, Mac thought, that parking a car like that in this neighborhood was just asking for it to get stolen. Mac was behind the wheel, tearing wires out from under the steering column before the Pierce Arrow was out of sight. Baring the wires with a pocket knife, he touched red to green. The engine revved, he hit the gas and swung the Marmon into the street already shifting into second gear.

A man in a blue suit and homburg hat came running out of a florist's shop, followed by a woman dressed for dancing. Both began to chase the car and wound up screaming in the street. The Marmon 16 was already around the corner.

The gang of bootleggers circled back to Lincoln and turned right on Ashland, headed through Chicago's Loop. Mac tried to keep two or three cars between him and the Pierce Arrow so he wouldn't be seen, causing him to almost lose them at a red light. He gunned the engine and caught up with them two blocks later. But before they reached Whiskey Row the bootleggers turned right on 43rd Street, the Union Stockyard, referred to by the locals as "Back o' the Yards."

"Hey, Boss!" one of the goons in the red Arrrow said. "I think somebody's followin' us!" He reached in his coat for his gun.

The small man with his hair parted in the middle slapped his hand down and laughed.

"In a Marmon 16?" he said. "Guy would have to be a complete moron to tail somebody in a car like that."

Luckily, they couldn't see Mac behind the wheel. The reformed criminal managed to somehow hit every green light, but stayed in back of the traffic pretending to look for an address. Problem was, with all the gigantic meat packing companies in the Back o' the Yards there weren't enough addresses.

He trailed them to a warehouse on 43rd Street, part of the Purity Meats Company. He parked the Marmon on the street the moment he saw them turn into the lot. Something itched at the back of his scalp. Another Pierce Arrow passed him with three men in the cab. Two of the men wore long-brimmed hats and worn clothes, almost like farmers or hobos. Every one of them gave him a dirty look. He didn't belong here.

In fact a number of cars were pulling up. The lot behind the warehouse was almost full. Mac noticed a distinct lack of Model-T's and more than a few luxury sedans. The Meat Packing Industry 'Back of the Yards' wasn't exactly known for its luxury.

Pulling his hat down low, he drifted the Marmon 16 down the street as nonchalantly as possible and made note of the address. He took a left, drove toward the lake and parked the car on Michigan Avenue where it would easily be spotted. He'd call the police from a drug store, and the couple he'd stolen it from would have it back by dinnertime, if they knew which palms to grease.

Mac hit the sidewalk at a solid pace and was half a block away from the drug store when he looked up from under the brim of his hat still thinking he was a free man. Then he saw the little boy standing in front of the drugstore.

Mac's gumshoes froze. The rest of his body went stiff and twirled in one place like a flagpole in high wind. His jaw dropped in a frown. His wide eyes went almost blank then narrowed.

Mac McCullough was no stranger to the streets. He'd grown up alone on them. He'd ridden the rails, learned how to fight, steal and then disappear. From Kansas City to Pittsburgh his name still meant something to a select few of the criminal world. He'd planned the smallest burglary to the biggest heist and always executed it like a professional. He'd worked with gun runners, rum runners, numbers runners.

He'd done a lot of running. He had a healthy fear of jail and death, but he certainly wasn't a coward.

Yet at this moment, Mac McCullough looked terrified.

The boy stood in the September sun under the orange awning of the Rexall Drug Store, wearing short pants with a long-sleeved dress shirt and oddly wide suspenders. The silent youth gave Mac a creepy smile, and waved a finger toward himself in the worldwide signal for "Come here." Then he bowed and his long dark bangs fell into his eyes.

Mac McCullough spun on one foot and headed in the other direction.

Dodging around a fruit cart on the corner of Ontario, the mechanical crossing flag waved green. But crossing from the other direction were two other men.

They were dark, at least six-foot four, well over two hundred pounds, all of it muscle. Both wore blue suits, mustaches bordering on handlebars, and walked in the manner of hunters. When they saw Mac they smiled at the exact same time. They could've been twins.

Mac turned around again and strode briskly in the other direction, looking all the while like somebody waiting to get shot in the back.

The two men looked at each other, shrugged, and casually caught up with just a few steps. Mac was about to break into a run, but they were already on him. They each grabbed one of Mac's elbows, lifted him off his feet and proceeded to carry him back toward the drug store, his legs still spinning beneath him.

"Oh, so is this how it's gonna be from now on?" Mac yelled. "Come on, guys! Give me a break! I've been really busy! I promise!"

The two men looked at him and shrugged, looked at each other, shrugged again, and kept walking.

They carried to him to a '32 Lincoln KB parallel parked on the street. It was a big car, roomy enough to sit six in back. The boy in the odd suspenders mutely opened the door, and the two warriors in suits rolled Mac onto its floor.

"Mr. McCullough, a knight can be either a defender or a mere chess piece. You, my little Knight of Cups, must be both."

"Y'know, for royalty's sake, I'd appreciate it if your boys there could stop tossing me around like last week's laundry. How you doing, Mirella?"

Mac looked up from his hands and knees into a face as old as the ages. Skin hung like wet parchment over a skull with a red and purple kerchief that dangled over her face like the hood of Death. Her hands moved slowly, shaking. Yet her eyes burned like frozen blue fires in the two black holes that surrounded them. When she smiled the back of the car filled with light and warmth.

"I am fine as long as you are Mr. McCullough. We have need of your services."

"No! Last time you needed my services I wound up fighting a mad scientist at the World's Fair. Guy killed about fifty people, almost killed me, and destroyed half the fair. You know damn well I barely got out alive."

"I never said you were unwise, Mr. McCullough. I said you were the Knight of Cups."

"And The King of Thieves, which just isn't possible. Sure, I try to make a buck, but lady, I'm struggling out here. Plus, take a look around, I'm not exactly on everybody's ten most wanted list either."

"A good thief wouldn't be," Mirella replied.

Mirella Herne first appeared in Mac's life only a few weeks ago at the World's Fair. She had predicted there were going to be horrors that day that only Mac could stop, and she had been right. Mirella believed Mac to be the living entity of The Knight of Cups from the Tarot, a knight on a noble quest that was destined to find either greatness or death. Part of a sect whose bloodline traced back over two-thousand years, Mirella also believed Mac was the King of Thieves, a reincarnation of the Gypsy who had stolen the fourth nail from Jesus' foot at the crucifixion, thus giving Gypsies the license to steal.

Mac wasn't big on the responsibility.

"My services," Mac paused to brush off his lapel, "belong to me, Mirella. I'll do good if I can, but—"

"There's a war coming, Mr. McCullough," she interrupted. "And we need to make sure you're on the wrong side."

●●●

In an alley beneath the train tracks where the streets meet, hidden in the shadows of a hotdog stand and a small rail yard, a high wooden fence barricaded the perimeter of a junk strewn, dusty lot. In stark contrast, an exquisitely detailed sign hung over the gate reading "Crankshaft's Car Repair and Sales." But what made the sign stand out wasn't the quality of the block lettering. It was the two-foot tall sign above it. The silhouette of a doughboy from the World War charging over a ribbon, his bayonet drawn. The ribbon read "369th Infantry Division," better known as The Harlem Hellfighters, the hardest fighting unit on the Western Front.

Crankshaft Jones was Mac McCullough's closest friend. He'd coached Mac on the sandlots playing baseball when he was a kid and, although Mac would never admit it, had probably been the only good influence on a boy headed for the wrong side of the tracks. He was a mechanical genius. Anybody who knew cars in the city of Chicago knew Crankshaft Jones. Nobody but Mac knew Crankshaft was also the Bagman's partner, the nameless "spaceman" with reflective goggles witnesses had spotted at the scene of the crime.

Mirella considered him to be both Mac's squire and mentor. The ace mechanic only accepted the squire position because she had promised him a profit. He was the captain of Mac's Armory.

Gathered in the secret underground garage beneath Crankshaft's dusty car lot, the small group sat around a table fashioned from an empty wooden spool of construction cable, drinking tea from a clay pot and cups with no handles. Mirella's cup seemed to roll in her hand as if it had a life of its own.

"Mr. McCullough, your path is written but forged in fading blood. There is a butcher leading a horde of butchers. You must dance with the cattle to kill a butcher."

"Lady, I can't even do the jitterbug."

Her two mysterious sons standing behind her like guards with their arms crossed, Mirella pointed to the southeast corner of the garage with a leathery withered finger. In the shadows a cot was laid out with a blanket over it and some pulp magazines lay on the floor.

"Still having odd dreams, Mr. McCullough? Sleepwalking?" Mirella asked. At the World's Fair she had asked Mac whether or not he went into trance states, and had discovered Mac sleepwalked, sometimes for days, waking up with knowledge of subjects he wouldn't normally have. Last time that subject had been Chemistry.

"Not for about a month," Mac said. "Back when this whole thing started."

"The speakeasy you were in this afternoon, you saw what happened." It wasn't a question, Mirella knew. "That same scene was re-enacted all over the north side today. Butchers, evil men fighting for power—like a swarm of butchers, but butchers, headed this way."

"So there's a new mob in town?" Crankshaft stared at his hand wrapped around a cup on the table, pretending not to be interested. Mac filled Crankshaft in on the hard sale he'd seen at Barney's (Bar and) Grill.

"Yeah, I saw it," Mac said. "Even thought about mixing it up, but bootlegging's just another business around here. Will be till Prohibition's over. Doesn't pay to fight with those guys. That's big money, huge, like taking on an industry."

"And you are a one man operation—" Mirella let the silence hang in the air.

"Yes—no—I mean. I mean nobody's a one man operation. It's just—less people, less problems. And those bruiser types come with a trunkful of problems. Besides, Frank Nitti's no slouch when it comes to the whole gangster thing. His guys will take 'em out. I don't do bootleggers."

"Ah, were it not for your carefree attitude, Mr. McCullough, I fear you would go insane."

"She's not alone," Crankshaft offered.

"Unfortunately, there are lives at stake here," Mirella continued. "You are aware of the effects of wood alcohol poisoning, are you not?"

Mac's eye's widened just a little, then he almost smiled. Mirella knew The Bagman's father had been murdered by the mob with the same poison.

"Still having odd dreams, Mr. McCullough?"

"Ethanol?" he said.

"Yes, they plan to take over, then dilute the quality of the liquor to save money. Many will be struck blind, others will die. And that's just if they are successful. One butcher has gathered the others, from other cities and states. These are hard times. Men have lost more than their measure, everything in many cases. Hard men who will do violent things for little and they have been gathered from across the plains."

"You're describing an army," Crankshaft said.

"That works cheap," Mac added. "So, if what you're saying is true, we'd still have to start small. Hit one speakeasy at a time, while Frank Nitti's characters hit the others. Imagine me, working with Frank Nitti? It stinks. Up to now he's just ignored me, and I kind of like it that way. He's got an army, too."

Crankshaft looked at Mirella, his dark brown eyes glancing as if to ask a question. The old crone nodded and smiled with her lips. Her presence in the secret underground garage seemed to affirm her acceptance of Crankshaft, and gave the warehouse-sized, underground lot an air of worldly knowledge.

Hey, smart guy." Crankshaft pointed a finger in the air. "What if for once in your life you didn't go in guns blazing?"

"Oh, I get it," Mac said. "You guys want me to become one of this gang of butchers, so I can steal their dough like I've been doing with Nitti's garbanzo beans."

Crankshaft looked away then glanced back in a double take. He hadn't expected Mac to get it that quickly. Or at least part of it.

"No, I think Mirella wants you to play spy, for real. She's not just talking about hit and run. She's talking about destroying an organization, a butcher's shop."

"You want me to move in with the new guys? A gang I know nothing about? Jeez, they could all be sadists or weirdoes or something. From what I've seen they're the leg breakin' type, the kind of guys you definitely don't want your sister going out with. And, the only way in with a gang like that is to start breakin' legs. Problem is a lot of people in the city know who I am—hell, half the civilians on the street. I can't exactly go out and start busting them up for the Butcher's Shop. I won't. And I don't have a disguise that's going to hold up for more than a week or two. I'm just not that good."

Mirella scoffed.

"C'mon, Kid, think. I've seen you commit crimes nobody ever even noticed," Crankshaft said. "And, I know you lived under aliases in Kansas City and Pittsburgh, and there's just got to be a way for a poor, dishonest man to get a job. You know, I hear 'prosperity is just around the corner.'"

Mac sighed a whoosh of air at the political catch phrase that had quickly become a cliché.

"Crank, in the criminal world, second-story and confidence men don't exactly run to give the mob ten per cent of their take, and, unfortunately, most of my crime experience lies in those two fields. I've got to figure out a way to get in without hurting a civilian."

Crankshaft slapped the hat off the top of Mac's head. Mac gave him a dirty look as he reached behind him and picked it up by the brim, then, without looking, tossed it on a ten-inch nail in the wall that posed as a hat rack.

"You don't have to, Mac. Don't you get it? Sure, everybody in the wrong part of town *thinks* you're still a crook, but every job you've heisted from Frank Nitti's mob you've managed to frame somebody else for, or been posing as somebody else. So—while you don't have to worry about fighting Nitti yet—as far as word on the street goes, you've never worked on a job linked to him."

"So you think they'll assume I have a bone to pick with Nitti and the Outfit?"

"That is what I meant when I said we had to get you on the wrong side, Mr. McCullough." Mirella chuckled to herself. The lights in the room seemed to flicker brighter.

Mac pushed his chair away and began to pace back and forth. Crankshaft knew that's how he thought best. Mirella stared into space as if waiting for something. Her sons stood poised like cigar store Indians.

"Huh," Mac murmured, under his breath, grasping his chin with his fingers and weighing his options. He paced a good three minutes, staring at the air above him, and then stopped in his tracks. "It's going to take some muscle."

"I am sure my sons Kerr and Tobar would be more than happy to provide you with some, Mr. McCullough." Mirella waved her hand at her sons behind her.

Mac smiled, as did the two gigantic brothers.

It occurred to Mac then that he knew Mirella and her sons were Travelers, Gypsies, but he had no idea what country they were from or what sort of lives they led. They kept a hideout in a curio shop in Greektown, but it was only open by appointment. Mac had never seen it open and he'd drifted by the address more than a few times since he had met the woman who believed him to be the King of Thieves. Regardless, what Mirella said was always the real deal, and her two sons made the local bruisers look like half-pints.

"You know where the head butcher lives?" Mac asked Mirella.

"I'm afraid you will have to find that out yourself, Mr. McCullough. Part of this adventure may find you on your journey as the Knight of Cups as well as the King of Thieves. One enables the other to become greater."

"So, no address," Mac said, completely ignoring any greater lesson involved. The only thing he knew about the legend of the Knight of Cups is that it was some kind of quest that might kill him. He didn't want to think about it.

"No," Mirella said. "No address, just muscle."

Kerr and Tobar stepped forward from behind Mirella, dwarfing everyone else in the room. One of them slapped Mac on the back and spoke.

"Knock, 'em dead, Yankee."

●●●

Mac hit the speakeasies for two nights. Not drinking much, but consorting with the underworld in its own habitat. None of the locals knew about the Butchers. He'd gotten a few narrow-eyed looks from some out-of-towners, though. New guys that didn't seem to mind the new beer as much as everybody else. Still, nobody said a word about anything to do with a new gang in town.

Then, early on the third night, he spotted Melvin Fleece.

Fleece was an accountant as good as his name. He had fleeced quite a few people, and probably a few states, with his accounting antics and short-term finance scams. He was a bit of a misfit, being neither mobster nor legitimate businessman. The little weasel had worked for Dominick Giambrone's mob in St. Louis, keeping his books. It must have ended on good terms. Fleece was still alive.

Mac had spent six months in St. Louis in the late twenties selling oil wells that didn't exist under the name of Larry Garvin. Larry had been the flashy kind of character in black tie and gold rings that Mac wasn't. These days Mac's fashion sense leant more toward blending in with the crowd than standing out. In his hometown he felt flashy wearing pinstripes.

Melvin sat leaning over the far end of the bar trying to look invisible. Mac crossed the room and sat down next to him.

"Well, if it isn't Mr. Fleece! Remember me, Melvin?"

Fleece twitched, almost broke and run. He was a little guy with a thin mustache. Mac grabbed him by the lapel before he could readjust himself in his seat and try to look innocent.

"Melvin from St. Louis, right? I'm Larry Garvin, y'know 'the Gar', remember?" Mac smiled his huckster's corn-fed conman grin.

Fleece squinted at him for a second, then smiled. His entire body visibly relaxed.

"Larry 'the Gar' Garvin! Man, you scared the crap out of me." He straightened his suit and picked up his drink. "I'm not exactly on good terms with the Feds these days. I haven't been called Melvin in quite a while." Having regained his composure, Fleece stopped to light a cigarette, lowered his eyebrows and tried to look tough. "So, what do you want, Garvin?"

"I haven't gone by Garvin in a long time," Mac said.

"I knew it!" Fleece snapped his fingers. "I always knew you was into some of the shady stuff, Garvin, even if I didn't let on. Hell, working for Giambrone it was just out of my line at the time."

"Name's Mac, Mac McCullough." He stood up and the two men shook hands.

"Ah, nice Irish name. Bet something like that works good for you in a town like this."

"It does." Mac waved at the bartender signaling for two more beers. "I'm trying to find something out," Mac said, as if he were on a spiritual quest rather than one for information.

"Well, ask away, Mac. Ask away." Fleece tapped the ash off his cigarette and spun his barstool so it faced his new friend. "By the way, the name's Mathews now, Bill Mathews." He winked.

"Well, what I was wondering, Bill— What I was wondering was—well, I've been looking for some quick dough."

"Aw, Cmon, Gar, I mean Mac," Fleece corrected himself. "Town like this was made for a quick buck. There's a million people here."

"Sure, sure. But I need to make a few dollars quick. And I won't work for Frank Nitti."

"That's your problem, buddy."

"Is it?"

Judging by the way he was edging onto the back of his seat, Melvin Fleece AKA Bill Mathews, didn't feel so comfortable anymore.

"What do you say, Melvin—Bill—whatever you're calling yourself these days. Who are you working for? Nitti? The Chamber of Commerce? The D.A.R.?"

"The D.A.R.?" Fleece took Mac seriously. He lowered his eyebrows and his head went back on his neck, curious.

Mac grabbed the accountant by the lapels and pulled Fleece off his seat, then grabbed him by one arm and dragged him to a corner booth in the shadows. Throwing Fleece onto the seat, Mac reached across the table and grabbed him by the tie so he couldn't run away.

"Spill it, Accountant, or I start withdrawing teeth. A guy like you doesn't just pop into town unless he's involved in a big operation. Who and what is it?"

"I can't tell you anything."

Mac grabbed the knot on Fleece's tie with his one hand started pulling it tight with the other. Fleece turned red then a little blue. Mac loosened the knot so the white-collar criminal could talk.

"I can't tell you who," he said between gasps for breath. "Because—nobody knows who—the boss man is."

"Then, who's his lieutenant? Y'know, his right hand man?"

Fleece wrestled with his collar like he was trapped in his shirt. Mac held the tie tight.

"OK, OK! Some little guy, little but tough. His name's Jake Madlin. They call him 'Grinder.'"

"Little guy? Blondish hair? Looks like he took his acting lessons from Cagney and Napoleon at the same time?"

"That's him. Always wears a double-breasted suit."

"He travel around with a guy in overalls and another guy in a new suit, who still looks like he just fell off the turnip truck?"

"The other guy in a suit is Curtis 'The Cleaver' Hatfield. He's crazier than Madlin, acts like he's bulletproof. The bruiser in the overalls is Dutch Webb, used to be a farmer down in Gary before he became a pro-wrestler."

"But he got kicked out for some reason," Mac said, "and now he's Grinder Madlin's hired muscle—"

"You got it." Fleece tried to wheedle Mac's hands off his tie knot. Mac held on.

"So, where can I find Grinder?"

"Half the speakeasies on the north side." Fleece tugged at his collar again.

"Sorry, all those speakeasies have 'No Salesmen' signs in the window." Mac tightened the tie's knot, and held on with a fist. He lit a cigarette with his other hand and leaned uncomfortably close to Fleece's pale skin with the lit end. "I need a home address, Melvin."

"Look, they're renting a bunch of houses, got a bunch a new mugs in town, but that's all I can tell you. These guys work on a need to know basis, and since all I do is count the beans, I never know anything till it's over."

"Hmmm." Mac's massaged his jaw with his hand, then grabbed Fleeces tie again. "OK. I get it. You think they have any entry level positions open?"

"Like I said, I don't really know."

"Oh, don't worry. It's all right, I get it." Mac signaled to the bartender for another round, then waved two fingers in the air, ordering them both shots of bourbon. "No hard feelings, Mr. Mathews, none at all."

Mac leapt from his seat to retrieve the drinks from the bar before somebody thought about carrying them over to the table. He set the drinks down and tossed the tray on top of a mismatched stack of trays on the corner of the bar, then sat down.

"Well, here's to the best laid plans of mice and mobsters!" Mac clinked his shot glass against Fleece's and gulped it in one swallow. He made a face, smiled at Fleece.

Fleece smiled back, downed his liquor and started sipping his beer.

Mac smiled and waved at the bartender for another round, got up a moment later and retrieved the drinks from the bar again.

"Y'know, Mathews, you're right! Guy like me, if I were to go back to the old con game in this city I could clean up." Mac slammed the glasses down on the table, and spun the tray through the air back on the corner of the bar. "Yeah, a guy doing the old 'magic wallet' con could go far in this town."

"That's the spirit!" Fleece tapped Mac's glass with his and drank the shot, again, sipping his beer afterward. "There's a lot of old cons you could get away with in this city. 'Course, I wouldn't zactly shay thish ish the place to try selling a gold brick." His speech was beginning to slur.

"No, those old cons are still the best. You just have to update them for the times. It's a modern crazy world we live in now. Hard for people to catch up. Gotta stay one step ahead of the other guy."

"You shaid it." The upper half of Fleece's body weaved in his seat. "Shay, did I ever tell you about wha' happened with the Giambrone mob in Shaint Louish?"

"No." Mac sipped his beer.

"No? Well let me tell you, Gar, that Giambrone wash one mean shon of a bitch. Toward the end there he wanted to kill me, but when he got hish handsh on the extra cash I'd stored away. Well, at first he wants to kill me. Then, then—" He belched. "Say, I—don't feel— I mean I'm feeling kinda—" He belched again. "—woozy. Think I better get shum air"

Fleece tried to stand up but couldn't. He fell back in his seat.

"Must've been those drinks. Haven't been out on the town too—much late—ly…" The dodgy little accountant gave Mac a wounded look. "Oh, no— you—didn't…"

Mac picked his own mug up and drank it to the bottom. He sat across the booth from Fleece watching his eyes fade as he sank in his seat.

Mac sold sundries at his cigar store. He had seen the sleeping pills available on the same form he used to order aspirin for the shop and bought a case of the things. Every sip of beer Fleece drank had been laced with sleeping pills Mac had pounded into a powder. The pills appeared to him to have been a nice addition to his inventory. They certainly had paid off this week.

He stepped around the booth and sat down on the opposite side, where he was in a position to hold Fleece up if need be. Fleece stared at the space in front of him blankly, his eyelids fluttering. Mac reached into the accountant's jacket and retrieved his wallet, grateful the weasely little numbers crusher didn't keep it in his hip pocket. Three hundred dollars in assorted bills were inside.

He'd checked the cash first. Old habits die hard.

Pulling out the remainder of the wallet's contents, he went through a handful of business cards and found one with a list of names and numbers on the back of it. Mac immediately stuck it in his vest pocket and then went through the rest of them. A fake I.D. in 'Mathews' name, cards for a bail bondsman, the Cosmopolitan Bank, a bookie, off track betting, a coin shop, and then, what he was looking for. A card for the Edward Hotel in the Back of the Yards neighborhood. There was an address written on the back and beneath that a name with an initial: J. Madlin. And, Madlin was the Butcher's lieutenant.

Mac stuck the card in his pocket and buttoned his jacket so his gun wouldn't show. He threw one of Fleece's arms behind his head and over his shoulders, so he could carry him like a fireman. Placing his right arm behind the nearly unconscious man, he put it beneath Fleece's right arm and slid him out of the booth. Holding Fleece's wrist with his left hand, Mac gripped the accountant's belt with his right, and carried him across the floor. Fleece tottered, while the big man balanced their way out, but somehow managed to remain respectably upright as Mac scuttled him toward the door. Mac turned.

"'Night all," he said, spinning full circle.

Fleece's hand waved limply at his side, slapping the door frame as they completed the revolution and lurched into the night.

●●●

Once outside, Mac threw the unconscious accountant over his shoulder and made his way down the sidewalk. Only two dim bulbs lit the block as Mac carried Fleece's limp body to a V-8 sedan he'd borrowed from Crankshaft's garage. The rear door opened for him and he slung Fleece inside. Kerr or Tobar, he couldn't tell which was which, grabbed the body by the lapels and pulled it onto the seat next to him. Mac scooted into next to Fleece. The Gypsy soldier gave him a sideways nod and an approving smile.

"We need to go to the 'Back o' the Yards', boys," Mac said. "We got something to prove."

"Knock 'em dead," the driver said.

Mac got it now. Tobar was the one that talked—sort of. Tobar hit the ignition, and the car twisted into the empty night.

"Now, let's just hope I can make the old 'magic wallet' con work in reverse."

The magic wallet was one of the oldest con games in the world. The entire scam rested on the victim finding the conman's "magic wallet," which was loaded with a respectable amount of cash and forged documents sanctioning the conman's scheme, endorsements and notes from prominent people, sometimes even letters from the President. Mac's plan was to use the accountant as his "magic wallet." And, since Fleece was unconscious, and an "old friend," he was the perfect pigeon to vouch for Mac McCullough's disrespectability.

●●●

'The Back of the Yards' was still officially called the Town of Lake, but it was already the Back o' the Yards to the locals. The Union Stockyard, Chicago's "hog butcher to the world" sat between 39th and 47th Street, originally south and west of the city. Then the city had grown around it. The Back of the Yards was home to Chicago's meatpackers. Contained within was an assortment of every nation that had ever sent an immigrant to the city, but mostly a collection of Slavs, with a smattering of Blacks and Jews on the edges.

The smell of steam, disinfectants, manure and blood mixed in the air, but was a lot more tolerable once it blended with the coal used for cooking and heat in the neighborhood. The address with Grinder Madlin's name written above it sat just off Halsted and Forty-Fourth, a thirty-year old three flat that had probably been thrown up right after the great fire.

Mac rapped on the door five times, a respectable salesman's knock.

He made a point to keep his hands away from his lapels, he had no idea what he was walking into and didn't want anybody opening the door and thinking he was reaching for a gun. Besides, his left hand was still holding Fleece upright by his belt.

He'd expected some squinty goon with a gun, but was greeted at the door by a young woman in a plain calico dress. She wore no makeup and kept her auburn hair in a short bob. Mac let go of Fleece's belt and wrapped his arm under the accountant's to hold him up.

"Uh, hi." Mac plastered his corn-fed con man grin on. "Bill Mathews had a little trouble making it home. I figured I'd help him, seeing as how I knew him back in St. Louis."

"Mr. Mathews?" The young lady's voice rang with surprise, but she was still smiling at Mac. "Well, I never would've suspected—Mr. Mathews drunk, not in a million years." That's when she noticed Mac was holding good ol' Bill up. "Oh, I'm sorry. Please, put him on the couch over there." She flung open the door and pointed into the living room.

Mac slung the drugged numbers juggler over his shoulder and carried him inside, glancing around the room to get an idea of the set-up. She was about to close the door, then the young lady's eyes widened. The young lady froze, standing still as Kerr and Tobar stepped out of the shadows and inside.

Two overstuffed chairs sat with their backs to the front window. A radio stood on a table by one wall, a couch on the other with the stairway next to it. The wall behind the couch had a medieval painting on it depicting a village butcher at the market, surrounded by legs of lamb and sausages hanging from a rack, while people fought for food in front in front of it. Mac thought it looked like one of those Hieronymus Bosch paintings where mutants had replaced all the usual skeletons and demons that tormented people in hell. Not the kind of thing you normally saw in the family room. Other than that, though, it looked like a regular boarding house set up. He lowered Fleece/Mathews onto the couch gently.

"Please don't think this is a common occurrence," the young woman said. "It's never happened before. Mr. Mathews is some sort of accountant. He spends most of his time upstairs writing numbers in columns and rarely goes out in the evening. Perhaps he felt the need to sow a few more wild oats than usual."

"Yeah, he put down a few for a little guy. I'm Mac McCullough by the way. These are my buddies Kerr and Tobar."

"Mara Madlin, pleased to meet you." She bowed, almost curtsying. "Can I get you some coffee, Mr. McCullough?"

"Please, call me Mac. And, no, you don't need to go to that trouble. I just wanted to make sure Melv—I mean Bill, got home all right." Mac had purposely slipped Fleece's real name.

"No problem at all, Mac. I've already got a pot on. You boys take cream and sugar?" Mara had already started walking toward the kitchen. Mac looked at Kerr and Tobar to see what they took. The two men stood like stone statues.

"Black is fine!" Mac said, through the kitchen entrance.

Mara came right back through the swinging door like the tray had already been prepared.

"Your friends can sit down, you know." She placed the cups in appropriate places on the table.

"I'm afraid the only adequate seating for them would be on the couch, Miss Madlin, and Mr. Mathews seems to have already filled that space. Besides, they're the kind of guys—if they really need anything, they usually get it."

The girl smiled instead of registering any kind of fear. Mac had unbuttoned his coat to let his gun show, slipped the wrong name and shown up with two large piles of hired muscle, and this girl hadn't flinched at all. She was either the most naïve woman he'd ever met, or the most hardboiled. Take her out of the baggy clothes, drop the cornpone accent a bit, and she could be attractive.

Mac stopped kidding himself. She was already attractive, even if it was just that cute girl-next-door look. Extremely attractive. Mac was practically smitten.

"So, you manage this boarding house?" he picked up his coffee and sipped it.

"My cousin actually owns the building. He rents out some rooms to friends, and I get to act as the housemother when I come home from my job at the plant. They're out most of the time. I get free room and board as long as I cook, and I can listen to the radio whenever I want. It's not too bad."

"Good coffee." Mac eyed the cup as he put it back on the table. "Doesn't sound like you're originally from around here."

"No, I'm from Kentucky. Went to visit Kansas City one time and never went back. Been here a few weeks. Saw the World's Fair, but I still haven't really had time to see the town."

Mac sighed; glad she'd seen the World's Fair. He'd had enough of it.

"Well, there are quite a few nice clubs in town, and a few not so nice places, both with and without alcoholic refreshment. I'd be glad to act as an escort. What are you doing, say, seven o'clock tomorrow night?"

"Oh, Mr. McCullough, aren't you the forward one." She still wore the smile. "I don't know, I don't normally—"

"I'll have you back home by eleven, and if you have to cook for the house I can wait as long as they can."

Seemingly in the background now, the structures called Kerr and Tobar grinned at each other. Mac gave them the eye and a brush off motion with his hand when Mara wasn't looking. One of them whispered in the others ear.

A door slammed upstairs, shoe heels scraped the steps, and a man's legs appeared briskly descending the staircase. The shoes shined like mirrors and the slacks were fine wool. When he reached the landing, a short blonde man in his shirtsleeves with his hair parted in the middle appeared. It was Grinder Madlin.

"Everything all right down here, Cousin?" he said, clipping the end of a cigar off with a silver cigar tool. "These guys aren't causing any trouble down here, are they?"

"Oh no, Grinder, honey. Not at all. Mr. McCullough here was just dropping off Mr. Mathews. Seems he's a little tight right now."

Grinder Madlin raised an eyebrow when he saw Kerr and Tobar and then lowered both of them in suspicion.

"Please, you can call me Mac." He stepped forward and held out a hand.

Madlin shook it grudgingly. "Grinder Madlin."

"And these two big guys are my cousins, Kerr and Tobar," Mac said. "Sorry, they don't speak much English, but they're good eggs. I promise."

Kerr and Tobar bowed their heads.

"Well, uh, thanks for bringing Bill home in one piece. We sure do appreciate it. Here—" He reached into his pocket and pulled out a wad of bills, skimmed three off the top and held them out in the air. "Let me give you something for your trouble."

He was giving Mac the bum's rush.

"If it's all the same to you, Mr. Madlin, I'd rather earn it." He glanced from side to side. "Can I talk to you for a second? Without our cousins around?"

Madlin's eyes narrowed to match his eyebrows.

"Mara, could you give us a minute?" Grinder pointed toward the steps.

Mac waved his jaw at Kerr and Tobar, and the two hulks stepped outside on the front porch. Mac and Grinder sat in the two remaining chairs. Madlin pulled a silver plated lighter out of his pocket and went to work on the cigar.

"What's the story, Buddy? You *do* look kind of familiar, but that's not always good in my business."

"And what business is that?" Mac said.

"Shipping, importing, exporting. You know, that kind of stuff."

"Stuff, huh? What kind of stuff?"

"Y'know, imports, exports."

Mac scoffed. "Look, back when I knew Bill Mathews here, his name was Melvin Fleece."

"I'm well aware Mr. Mathews changed his name. He works for me. It's legal and there's been nothing suspicious about the work he's done. People do it all the time. Look at Hollywood."

"Yeah, except back when I knew him in Saint Louis, my name was Garvin, and Melvin there is not exactly the Hollywood type."

Madlin stopped playing with his cigar, looked up at Mac with a curious grin on his lips.

"Waitaminute! I recognize you!" Grinder Madlin said. "You're that guy from the little two-by-four speakeasy!" He edged off the seat and his right hand dangled too close to the gun under his lapel. "What'd ya do, follow me here?"

Mac backed in the other direction, trying to look as intimidated as possible. The best actors Hollywood could offer had nothing on the veteran confidence man.

"No! No, Mr. Madlin. Believe me, if I'd known it were you I probably wouldn't be knocking on your door. But I do know my way around this city—and I've always managed to earn a less-than-reputable buck around here. I take orders well, and I have no illusions about the chain of command. I like to stay alive, see."

"Yeah, I see." Madlin said, eyeing Kerr and Tobar through the window. "You always take your own hired muscle around with you?"

"No, they really are my cousins. Distant relatives, but cousins. In fact they don't have to be involved at all, unless you want 'em. One thing—you don't have to worry about 'em talking."

"I see—" Madlin clenched his jaw then rubbed it with his hand. "So, how am I supposed to know you're not working for some other mob? Just playing me for a patsy?"

"Ask around. Mac McCullough has been involved in enough shady deals in this city that people—including the Outfit—are bound recognize my name."

"Nah, I need something more." Madlin eyed him seriously and knocked the ashes off the end of his cigar into the ashtray on the table in front of him.

"How about the inside track on a fur robbery?" Mac said.

Madlin's eyes widened and a big-toothed grin broke out across his face. It was the first time Mac had ever seen him smile. It was the smile of an overpowering ego backed by an erratic mind.

"Fur! Now that's more like it! Personally, just between you and me," Madlin lowered his voice and talked across the back of his palm, "I been concentrating on the bootleg business because it's the quickest way to the top. But we been pressing some of you local boys for ideas on how to expand ourselves in this burg, and you're the first to come up with anything. Your job?"

Mac hated to weasel Mr. Quirt out on the fur deal, but he had been forced to hunt for food in his early hobo days and had since gained a great respect for animals. Even chickens, which he thought were the dumbest animals in the world, were hard to steal from a farm without squawking. Besides, he had been going to steal most of Quirt's dishonest money to begin with, and if it had worked out like he'd planned, Mac would've ended up taking most of the cash anyway.

"Yeah, it's my job," Mac lied. He knew nothing about the set up, but he had to convince Madlin that his mob would get a bundle. Mac decided then to offer a percentage like a good crook. "Got it all laid out and going into the final stages."

"How much you expect to net?"

"Twenty grand, after we fence them. Split four ways, that's six grand apiece. And two-thousand dollars for you! Tax-free, just for sitting back and letting us do it."

"And how do I know you're not one of Frank Nitti's bums? Seems like a lot of free cash for you to just come waltzing in here with."

"I waltz because I love the dance, Mr. Madlin—I do love the dance. Bottom line is, I been giving this a lot of thought for a long time. I mean, there's longer term profit in booze than there is in heists. And, when the geniuses in Washington finally get their act together and repeal Prohibiton. Well, I guess that's when guys like you—and hopefully me—get to move on up to Respectable Street, if you know what I mean."

Madlin massaged his jaw again and seemed to eye Mac with a little more respect, most likely because the little mobster had come to the realization that Mac was smarter than he looked. That or he simply planned to use the Chicago native and bury him later.

"So, a smart guy, eh," he said.

"Not too smart. I want to live past Prohibition."

"But you want to be respectable, too. You probably won't live long enough."

Mac stared respectable knives into Madlin's eyes. Madlin stared back like he was trying to break his eyes away, but couldn't.

"Ask around," Mac said, unmoving. "Dare me, even."

"Done. You got brass, kid. Give me a call day after tomorrow, if I don't call you. But if I find out you're not in," Madlin made a slashing symbol across his own throat, "You may be on your way out."

"Thanks." Mac smiled, and handed him a card with a number on the back of it. If the gangster checked, he would have found out the number was for Barneys (Bar and) Grill, the same speakeasy he'd rousted when Mac was there.

Madlin stubbed out his cigar in the ashtray, turned toward the steps, then stopped. He turned back around to see Mac still standing in the living room. He'd expected the big guy to let himself out. Mac shuffled his feet. Madlin lowered an eyebrow and gave him a look asking why he was still there.

"Um, could I speak with Mara a minute?" Mac said. The tough guy look had faded and he'd gone back into turbo-rube.

Madlin's look changed to curious. He yelled Mara's name up the stairs, and began standing around, shifting his feet, waiting to see what happened.

Mara came whooshing down the stairs, her hand on the bannister, her skirt full of air from the quick descent. She stopped and stood on the landing.

"See you tomorrow at seven, Mara?" Mac said.

"Why yes, Mr. McCullough. It would be a pleasure."

"Pleasure's all mine." Mac opened the door behind him and exited without even looking where he was going.

Madlin looked at Mara, then back at the door thinking about the "smart guy."

•••

"Mac smiled and handed him a card..."

Damned if Madlin didn't call the next day.

Popeye sent a kid over to the cigar store, and for once Mac actually happened to be there. The Napoleonic mob boss wanted Mac and the boys to pop in on a speakeasy on the near west side called The Dot and tell them they were a "new customer."

The Near West Side was historically an important port of entry for immigrants. The neighborhood was predominantly Italian with some Greeks and Jews, but in the last ten years a Latin population had begun to congregate along Halsted south of Hull House. The Dot sat just down the block and had a reputation for late night fights and sexual shenanigans.

A large wooden three-flat painted white, the speakeasy looked like the kind of house a little old lady might live in. Sure enough, Mac looked up to see a wrinkled female senior citizen peering out the highest window. The old broad was either a prisoner, somebody's relative, or making at least five-hundred bucks a month rent-free.

They drove the V-8 to the alley around back and parked on the grass next to a driveway on the opposite side of the street. With the engine still running, Mac, Kerr, and Tobar stepped out of the car. The three lumbered toward the garage in back of the house. Tobar gave Mac a questioning look.

Mac pulled a ring of keys out of his coat, looked at Tobar then the lock. He had a lock-pick set in a small leather case in his coat, too, but if he had the right key, he could pull off the job a lot faster. It was the same lock that had come with the old wooden door. It clicked open with the first key he tried. Mac shooed Kerr and Tobar off to the side where they couldn't be seen and jerked the creaky garage door up.

Inside, surrounded by a few dozen kegs of beer, stood two men in brown leather jackets and flat caps. They would've looked like dock workers, but the fall weather wasn't cool enough for the leather. The jackets bulged with guns near their shoulders, and, they wore ties.

"Hi, guys." Mac waved.

"What do you want?" The one on the left said.

"For nobody to get hurt," Mac announced, but his eyes held an evil gleam.

Both men strode over, crowding him. The one on the right pressed his gun barrel against Mac's head.

"Only one here in any danger of gettin' hurt is you," he said.

Kerr's enormous fingers pinched the man's gun hand like he was using a pair of tweezers. Tobar held the other man in the air by the back of the collar. The Gypsies covered the gunmen's mouths with their free hand. Both never stopped smiling.

The brothers searched the men's coats. The guns clattered on the concrete floor of the garage. Mac picked them up, twirled a .45 automatic around his finger, and piled them behind one of the kegs. Kerr and Tobar tied the gangsters up, using their own belts and shoelaces to bind them and gagging them with their ties.

Mac snaked his way to the speakeasy's back door entrance and pulled the revolver from his shoulder holster. The door was unlocked. Mac eased it open, peeked through the crack and the edges of his lips turned up.

Guarding the door was a Latino man a little over six-feet tall. Wide shoulders stood over a stout belly. Mac was smart enough to realize that belly fed a whole lot of muscle because that belly belonged to a man named Gomez. Gomez wasn't his real name, but everybody called him that. Word on the street was if you saw him, you better "go-go Gomez." Rumor had it that a man had once stolen a stable nag from him, and he'd killed an entire family trying to get his horse back. The last barroom brawl he'd been in, he'd cleared the room with a knife and stayed in the bar drinking. The cops didn't even bother him.

No wonder Madlin had wanted Mac to hit this place. But the little mob boss knew nothing of Mac's past or how broad it had actually been.

Gomez's real name was, Carlos Herrera. His family had been devout Catholics when they had died. That's how Mac had met him in the orphanage before they escaped together.

"Carl," Mac whispered.

"Mac? Mac McCullough?" Gomez opened the door wide.

Mac half-closed it again.

"I need your help, Go-go," he said. "C'mere."

Go-go Gomez approached warily. Mac kept whispering.

"I'm running a scam on some new bootleggers. You know the routine. The new guys come in with the muscle and tell you you're ordering your booze from us. You know what always happens. Want to make three-hundred dollars?" Three hundred dollars was a lot of money in 1933.

"Last time you offered me money," Gomez said, "I almost got in a lot of trouble."

"Got out of the orphanage, didn't you?"

"Been in trouble ever since." He smiled at him.

"Just keep it to yourself. These new guys can't last too long. Of course, you and I know nothing about that. Got it?"

"A man can earn a lot of money in this town not knowing a thing." Gomez grabbed the roll of bills out of Mac's hand. "Of course, if I should learn something—"

"Knock it off, Go-go. You know I'm always up to something; this something just happens to help you and Nitti's guys. Although, I'd rather you didn't tell Nitti that."

"He might just kill me."

"No he won't. You'll be knocked unconscious and making more than some of the fighters at the Marigold Gardens.

Gomez smiled and nodded, which was saying a lot for the close-mouthed Latino. It was all the guarantee Mac would get.

"Thanks, Go-go. You mind making a little dramatic entrance?"

●●●

The front room of The Dot was almost empty. It was still early in the day and the entire crowd consisted of five men gathered around the pool table and the bartender.

Carl "Go-go" Gomez ran three steps backwards into the room and launched himself onto the pool table like he'd been hit by a wrecking ball. The table stood firm as Go-go's three-hundred pound frame landed on it. Then it shook, and two of the legs gave way as he lay prostrate on the green felt. Go-go kept his eyes closed, pretending to be unconscious.

Three of the men stood gaping at Go-go's limp form. Only the bartender and one other man looked up at the back door. The bartender saw Mac's revolver and began to reach beneath the bar.

He wasn't washing glasses.

Mac barreled across the room faster than a man his size should be able to. Leaping over the bar with both feet in front of him, his shoes pounded the bartender directly in the chest and bounced him off the top shelf liquor. Mac surfed the body down the wall to the floor as a waterfall of bottles and mirrored glass showered over them. The Criminal Detective wound up behind the bar balancing on the man's ribcage.

"Now here's where I normally make the speech about nobody getting hurt," Mac said, as if he'd done it a thousand times. "But this guy wouldn't listen!"

The men around the pool table looked deservedly confused. Mac's other hand came up with a sawed off shotgun, and two of them put their hands up. Go-go moaned, giving Mac a chance to walk around the bar.

"Any of you guys work here?"

Two of the men shook their heads. The other two looked at their feet.

"Anybody know anybody that works here?" He grabbed one of the men that had been looking at their feet.

The man closed his eyes and turned his head, expecting a punch or worse.

"Don't worry, Buddy. We're not here to hurt anybody," Mac said. "We come bearing beer and whiskey."

The three other men seemed to exhale and visibly relax. The one Mac held stopped churning his feet, but still wouldn't open his eyes. Mac dropped him. Unprepared, the man's feet fell out from under him and he toppled onto the floor.

"Tell the owner, the bartender, whoever you have to—you've got a new liquor distributor. I know this might cause some problems with your current inventory, but in the long run it's a lot less bother. *Comprendé*?"

The men made eye contact with everything in the room but Mac. Mac wound up his leg like he was going to kick the man on the floor in the belly.

"*Capiche*? *Savvy*? Get it?"

The four men's heads bobbled like pistons in the affirmative.

"Lesson over. See you guys before the weekend."

Mac stepped through the back door. Kerr and Tobar slapped him on the back. Mac got behind the wheel. Kerr sat next to him, Tobar in back.

"Well, that was easier than I thought it would be. Thanks for letting me handle it. Makes me look better for the little mob boss."

"Knock 'em dead, Yan—"

Suddenly the windshield popped. Then they heard the gunshot. Cracks ran through the glass giving Mac and the crew a kaleidoscopic view of the intersection. Kerr and Tobar ducked beneath the windows. Mac leaped out of the car and rolled across the edge of the alley into a loading dock. His gun was in his hand.

There was a brief silence. Then Kerr and Tobar stepped outside. Tobar dashed for the loading dock, keeping his head low. Kerr stood at the edge of the alley sniffing the air like he was bulletproof. He pointed at a four-story building on the northeast corner and bounded down the alley zigzagging his way toward it. Mac saw a gray figure in a mask on the roof turn and run.

He chased the after the gray figure with Tobar right behind him. By the time they'd reached the building Kerr was out of sight. Inside, Mac glanced left and right, saw the sign for the stairs and took them two at a time. When he'd pulled his gun again and kicked the door to the roof open, Kerr was the only one there. The Gypsy warrior pointed to a rope dangling from the back of the roof to the alley behind it.

The gray figure ran east down the alley. It seemed to blend in with the shadows that stood out in the midday sun, disappearing and reappearing even further away. Mac grabbed the rope and half-climbed, half-slid down it. His eyes widened when he hit the concrete and Kerr was already standing there. Then Tobar showed how it was done.

Without prompting, without a care on his face—and without a net—Tobar leapt across the alley, grabbed an opposing balcony, swung from that to a drainage pipe and slid down it, hitting the earth already running toward the mysterious gray figure.

Mac made a mad dash ahead of them then stopped at the next intersection, his head spinning, searching. He spun for moment, and then raised both hands, before slapping himself in the head with is right.

"Damnit! Being chased is always easier than chasing somebody! All they have to do is keep running and turning."

Kerr sniffed the air, looking around, and pointed down the street as if to say "they went thataway."

"C'mon," Mac said, urging them to follow the mysterious gray figure.

Kerr tsk-tsked with his head and pointed at his watch. They were too late.

"You think it was one of Nitti's guys?"

The brothers shook their heads, saying "no."

"Yeah, that would be too fast. But who the hell would want to shoot at *me*?"

Kerr and Tobar doubled up laughing.

•••

Mac dropped Kerr and Tobar off around the corner from Crankshaft's lot on Lincoln Avenue. The normally stoic big boys were still like tourists to Chicago's Loop, pointing out the sites, joking and laughing in their own strange language. Mac pointed out a tailor and told them they might want to get some new suits. He still had to report to his new "boss."

Of course, before he could do that he had to borrow another car from Crankshaft. Luckily for Mac, it was after hours. He picked the lock on the gate. It was a game he and Crankshaft played. Mac kept picking the locks and Crankshaft kept changing them. Mac exchanged the decimated Model-A for a '32 Hudson Terraplane, without once wondering what Crankshaft's response would be to finding the shot-up remains of a Model-A in the middle of his lot the next morning.

•••

Madlin opened the door smiling. He waved Mac in and slapped him on the back.

Dutch Webb, the ex-wrestler, and his immense biceps sat on one side of the room, leaning off the edge of the couch. He looked like he was dressed for the gym now, having shed his overalls for khakis, a sweatshirt and tennis shoes. Curtis 'The Cleaver' Hatfield held up a drink, toasting from behind the wet bar, unbuttoned the coat of his suit and sat down across from Dutch Webb.

"Strong as you came on I didn't think you could do it, kid," Madlin said. "But you're all aces. Had my guys check out the club about an hour ago. Heard you knocked some big Mex dizzy."

"My pleasure," Mac said. "Go-go's an old friend of mine."

"Yeah, I bet you're real pals. Here, grab yourself a drink," he pointed at the wet bar, "and we'll get down to business."

Mac stepped over to the bar and mixed himself a respectable whiskey and soda. Madlin sat down on the couch next to Dutch Webb. Mac fell into a lounging position in an overstuffed chair, his legs extended and crossed under the coffee table.

"Like I said, ya done good, kid. I took the time to ask around. Not that too many people said anything about you, but I can tell you're a smooth operator. You could go far in this organization."

The sudden realization of an old fear hit Mac. He'd been forced to become the Bagman to escape from the Chicago Outfit and had been at war with them ever since. Joining another mob would be like signing his death warrant. He had to play it cool and loose. He had to join, without joining. It was exactly the kind of paradox that appealed to Mac's strange nature, his elastic morals and love of the grayer areas between the black and white—but there was no way in hell Mac McCullough would ever join any organization. Not even the Elks club.

"Sorry, Mr. Madlin, but I only work on contract. I don't want to take over the city; I just want to pull a profit out of it. I muscled in on that speakeasy, free of charge, so you'd know I don't kid around. You put me in on a job, I might let you know of a few others you could horn in on, and we'll both get what we want."

"Friendly business, huh?" Madlin's eyes narrowed. "Y'know, with the economy the way it is, most guys would leap at the chance I'm talking about. Hell, I pay room and board, a straight percentage on every job, and a hell of a lot of fringe benefits."

"I already have a place to live, and fringe on all the lampshades there."

Madlin rubbed his chin then sipped from his drink. He set it on the tabletop and turned the glass with his palm above it like he was trying to swab a ring onto the table's wooden finish, then sat back and stared at it.

"OK," he said. "You scratch my back, I scratch yours. You scratch it wrong, you're a dead man."

Mac didn't make threats. Instead, he stood up, reached across the table and shook Madlin's hand. Madlin swept his palm away

"One more thing," the little Napoleon said. "I got a job tonight I need you to work."

"Kind of short notice."

"Is this about the dame?" He thumbed over his shoulder upstairs.

'The dame?' It took Mac a second, but then he realized Madlin was talking about his cousin, Mara. "Well, yeah. That was part of it, but I have things to do."

"Yeah, well you got something else to do tonight, work."

Mac's eyes scanned the room. Everyone in it stared back at him. Eyes narrowed, and Kurt "The Cleaver" displayed a sideways smile. Mac sat up in his seat.

"Mara around?"

"Nah, she had to go downtown for something. Don't know when she'll be back. You can always leave a note."

"OK, you got me. Here's the deal, though. Do I have time to at least go get her some flowers first?"

"Flowers?" Dutch scoffed.

"C'mere." Madlin stood up, snapped a finger and waved for Mac to get up and follow him into the kitchen. Mac took his time. Madlin shut the door behind them.

"I want to talk to you about Mara. She may be my cousin, but the woman is trouble, especially around here. I don't want any woman trouble with this gang, see. Mara doesn't know anything that's going on around here. She thinks we're running a boarding house for meat packers. She's an out-and-out civilian and does what she wants, but you pull anything out of line, I'll rip your arm off and feed it to you."

"Another reason it's better for me to work on contract. I won't be around to cause the gang any 'woman trouble.' Look, Mr. Madlin, it's just a date. She seems like a nice young lady."

"You'll have to wait and see. I'll tell her we had business. You can leave a note and send some flowers later."

"All I have to do to get flowers is step outside. I got a bouquet in my car. Let me just go get them, and I'll leave them with a note."

Madlin nodded OK, guided Mac firmly toward the front door, and pushed it open. Dutch and Kurt "The Cleaver" eyed the new man suspiciously as he waved with his jaw and stepped outside to retrieve the flowers from his car.

"Odd little warning," Mac thought, skirting across the shadows of two lawns on his way to the sidewalk. Old habits like standing in the dark died hard. Skulking his way back to the rear of the Terraplane, he didn't realize anyone was in the car until he opened the door. Without thought Mac reached for his gun.

Then he realized it was Mara. Wearing smoked eyeglasses with a scarf wrapped around her head, she sat in the passenger seat, holding a bouquet of blue carnations in the lap of a stylish dress that looked like she had been poured into it. Her left leg extended from a slit in the skirt across the floorboards, like she might just pour out of it.

Mac exhaled the breath he'd been holding, and his hand came out of his jacket holding a pack of cigarettes. He held the pack out to her with two cigarettes extended just like in the movies.

Mara laughed and kept laughing as she spoke. "No, thank you. That has got to be the quickest recovery I've ever seen. I didn't mean to startle you, but that turned into quite the man-about-town-playboy reaction if I've ever seen one."

Mac wondered if she knew he'd been reaching for a gun. Leaned up against the outside of the car, put one of the cigarettes in his mouth and lit it.

"Yeah, I'm a real man of the world," he said, sliding into the driver's seat. "I see you got your flowers."

"Thank you so much. You really didn't have to."

"Well, given the situation, I almost wish I hadn't," Mac said. "I kind of have to work tonight."

"For my cousin Jake? That's not work." She put an arm on around Mac. "C'mon, you're going out with me."

"I don't think he'd like that idea too much."

"Which is why we're going to do it. Look, Grinder went so far as to send me out to the produce stand when the house was already full of fruits and vegetables. You and I both know he's all mobbed up, and if you're going out with him tonight that means you're probably just going to get into trouble. Come on, I'll tell him you kept me from going out with a cop."

"Look, I was just going to do some work for him," Mac said. "You really think he's all that mobbed up?"

"He likes to think he is, just like he *likes* to think I don't know anything about it. I don't know everything, but I certainly know he's not the boss. And, he'll do what I say."

"Will he?" Mac smiled. "Let me guess. You're side of the family has all the money."

"Something like that. Now drive before they come out and force you to play cards and smoke cigars all night."

Mac looked at Grinder's three-flat, then at the girl. He smiled again and started the engine.

•••

"So, do you come here often?" Mara asked.

"Never," Mac said. "This is a respectable place."

Mara laughed and had to cover her face with a napkin. They were just finishing dinner.

After leaving Grinder's place, Mac had taken Mara out for a few drinks at a speakeasy a little more respectable than the kind he usually went to, and then to the luxurious Edgewater Beach Hotel.

The Edgewater was the closest thing Chicago had to a vacation resort on the beach. Over three-thousand meals a day were served to the kind of people important enough to need a business district fifteen minutes from the beach. The hotel had its own radio station, WEBH, and was broadcasting Wayne King's orchestra that evening, live from their world famous outdoor dance hall on the beach. Mac had called in a few favors to get tickets to the broadcast and an extra favor, for a dinner reservation at the hotel's world famous Marine Dining Room.

In other words, he was out of his element.

The room sat one hundred people easily, with a dance floor in the middle and an entire wall of windows in back viewing the beach. The place was packed with celebrities, local dignitaries, and tourists also having dinner before the broadcast, some in evening dress.

Mac had waved at the waiter, signaling for the check and a cigar, and now he was the one waiting.

"I wouldn't worry too much," Mara said. "If things get too respectable for you, I'm sure we can always dance our way out to the beach and around some hobo's campfire."

"Yeah, but the food wouldn't be as good or the company."

Mara reached across the table and placed her hand on top of Mac's. He hadn't even realized he'd complimented her.

"Speaking of the beach," he said, "what's say we take a little stroll before dancing, it's nice out."

"OK, but I'm warning you. If I end up doing the Lindy Hop to some bum playing the harmonica on the beach instead of Wayne King, I'm probably not going to like it very much."

"I promise you won't even have to do the soft shoe. I just like people one-on-one more than in crowds, and this bunch needs to be herded. Plus, we can always sneak back onto the dance floor from the beach."

"Why sneak, you have tickets?"

Mac opened his mouth to answer, but never had the chance.

The double doors in front of the dining room slammed open so hard the walls shook. Three men with kerchiefs across their faces stepped into the dining room. Their actions were quick, professional, and rehearsed.

One stood with a .38 Colt Automatic in the doorway blocking it. One swept toward the right of the room with a Thompson Sub-machinegun. The other swept to the left with a second Tommy gun. In the back of the room, four more men with machineguns and covered faces appeared, two for each exit on every side of the dining room. They even had the bathrooms covered. A short man stepped toward the center of the dance floor and announced from under the kerchief covering his face.

"Hands up, ladies and gentleman! This is a robbery!"

Mac was reaching for his shoulder holster when he heard a scream from the back of the room. He glanced over to see a man who had been about to do the same thing. His hand was pinned to the table by a knife sticking out of it. Blood spread slowly across the tablecloth.

A wild-eyed man with a kerchief over his face laughed. Holding the man's arm down with one hand and pulling the victim's automatic from his shoulder holster, the grinning gangster held the gun up to the crowd as his victim struggled with the handle of the knife sticking out of his hand.

"Do not even think about guns, you dopes!" the apparent leader with the .38 said. "Look around. You want some stray shot taking out the city's finest citizens? I don't think so. Now, you be nice, and we'll be nice and quick. You get smart—"

The grinning gangster across the room's hand came out from under his lapel swinging a meat cleaver. In one downward motion the man with his hand pinned to the table lost all his fingers. Blood pulsed across the table. The crowd screamed with the victim. Men clutched their wallets, women clutched their pearls, and members of both sexes fainted. Somebody stood up, and two shots rang out.

A man in evening wear slumped to the dance floor bleeding from the head.

"Anybody makes trouble gets it!" The short robber said, brandishing his pistol. "Understand?"

Other than the occasional whimper, the crowd went quiet. Everything stopped. Then, people began to empty their pockets, almost in shock. The gang of masked men made their way around the tables, filling their bags with loot and monitoring the doors.

But when Mara Madlin glanced back across the table, her date had disappeared. While the rest of the crowd had been watching the violence, Mac was already sliding under the table and skulking toward the entrance.

He had recognized the voice of two of the armed robbers. It was the voice of his new gang. It was obvious that Kurt Hatfield—Jake Madlin's hired muscle—was the man with the cleaver, and the short statured leader was Madlin himself.

This had been Madlin's plan for the evening.

Mac was suddenly glad he'd gone on a date for more reasons than one. It was one hell of a daring raid, and "the Cleaver's" little show had stunned the entire crowd into silence. Given the economic status of the crowd, Madlin's gang could work ten minutes and make thirty-thousand dollars. Not a bad haul, but reckless.

And Mac McCullough knew all about reckless.

Kneeling to avoid the machine-gunners' eyes, his fingers clasped the silk-lined mask in his pocket as he slunk toward the door behind a small group of waiters frozen by the wall. One of the waiters jumped, suddenly aware of somebody behind him. Somebody else pushed back and the crowd shifted.

"What's going on over there?" Jake Madlin muttered, from behind his mask as he wedged his gun between two of the waiters to part the tiny crowd. Something snatched the gun from his hand and his eyes went wide. Madlin froze and began to back up slowly, the barrel of a .45 Colt Snubnose pressed directly between his eyes. Before he had a chance to move, Madlin found himself in a headlock with a gun to his temple.

"The Bagman." Someone in the crowd gasped the name the split second Curtis Hatfield had spat it.

Laughter rose from the floor to fill the high ceilings of the Marine Room till the wall of beachfront windows rattled in back. It wasn't happy laughter. It was the laughter of madness. The prankster wasn't merry, he was maniacal.

Madlin's goons turned just in time to see their boss being used as a human shield. Cursing, several raised their guns and aimed. Mac pulled Madlin higher, but realized at the same time the gangsters just might shoot their boss. If they opened fire in the restaurant it would be a massacre. He had to find a way to draw them away from the crowd.

Mac grabbed a handful of Madlin's hair and dragged him toward the lobby entrance. Rounding the corner, he heard those familiar words.

"Get him!"

The blood chilling laughter echoed down the hall, freezing the pulse of the bystanders. Avoiding the lobby, Mac loped down the hallway toward the dance hall, dragging Madlin behind him backward by the hair. Every time the tough little mob boss tried to turn and stop him, Mac pulled on his hair and he spun around again, cursing and spitting at the masked man.

Around the second corner, the Bagman stopped. Two icy blue-gray eyes stared so hard into Madlin's the gangster physically shrank. The Man of Steal slammed Madlin's head into the wall, hard, and waited with his gun in his hand.

Curtis "The Cleaver" Hatfield led the gang down the hallway, his mouth working as fast as his legs.

"That dumb son of a bitch thinks he can stop a mob, he's got—"

BLAM! Mac shot him in the thigh as Hatfield rounded the corner. Hatfield screamed like a girl and fell down, rolling on the carpet. Mac hurled himself down the hall cackling and yanking the stumbling Madlin behind him as the rest of the gang gave chase.

The hotel's "dance floor under the stars" was just around the corner. The Bagman may have looked crazy leading the gangsters from a small crowd to a larger one, but outdoors he'd have an advantage, and the crowd on the dance floor could run. Not to mention, there was a radio broadcast going on.

Two shots blasted behind him. Several people in the dance hall had already begun walking warily toward the beach, when Mac burst through the door and slung the nearly unconscious Jake Madlin at the band leader.

Madlin crashed into Wayne King's arms, and both men fell into the wood-wind section.

Mac jumped onto the edge of the stage as Madlin's gang rushed into the room. Grabbing the microphone from the announcer, he yelled as loud as he could at every listener in the greater Chicago area.

"Call the cops! There's an armed robbery at the Edgewater Beach Hotel!"

A Thompson and two automatics pointed at the band. Mac threw the microphone at the man with the Tommy gun and dived behind the drummer. The man with the machinegun put it to his shoulder, but Dutch Webb slapped it down. He'd heard The Bagman's announcement go out over WEBH and knew the police were already on their way. He turned, realizing he was surrounded by an unpredictable, shifting crowd. Some of them with guns.

"Forget it! Come on! We gotta get outta—"

Webb barely managed to get his hand up in time. One of the drum kit's cymbals bounced off his arm and crashed across the side of his head. He staggered and swayed, almost blacking out, waving his gun and backing toward the beach.

"Oh, c'mon! You guys started it!" The Bagman stood behind the now-empty drum kit brandishing another cymbal in his hand. A wave of ducking musicians parted in front of him.

One of the goons fired twice and grabbed Madlin as the gang reassembled itself by the wall. Part of the crowd screamed, part ran for the beach. A siren sounded, winding itself higher in the distance as others joined its chorus.

But when they looked back up at the bandstand, The Bagman had vanished.

"Keep your back to the wall, we'll go out to the beach and around the hotel," Dutch Webb said. Grinder Madlin was still clasping his head and walking in circles. Another man helped Curtis the Cleaver limp up from behind. The rest of the gangsters kept their guns out, and, pushing through the crowd, dashed for the sand. The men in the rear pivoted their heads back and forth searching for the Masked Madman who seemed to be everywhere and nowhere at once.

But The Bagman wasn't there.

The moment Mac hit Dutch Webb with the cymbal, he had jumped off the back of the bandstand. Seeing Madlin's mob head for the beach, he sprinted back inside through a screened porch behind the bandstand.

Hurtling through the kitchen to burst into the hotel lobby, The Bagman suddenly stopped.

He realized he had to let them get away. As much as he hated to, he had to. He'd wasted enough time just meeting the people at the top of this criminal heap and he didn't want to waste even more introducing himself to the people that replaced them. He had to let them get away. He'd kept people from getting robbed. He'd introduced The Bagman to Grinder Webb's gang. He regretted not telling them to get out of his city, but The Bagman had done his job.

Now it was time for the conman. Passing a long line of stoves and cooks that seemed to take no notice of him, Mac peeled off his hat, mask and tie. He tossed the hat and tie into the garbage by the swinging door, then burst through the lobby back outside, to head off Grinder and his gang.

Mac hit the sidewalk and began to slowly stroll under the awning toward the beach.

Dutch Webb, Grinder Madlin, and three more of their gang rounded the corner right in front of him. Their guns went up before they went down. Webb's eyebrows lowered in anger at his own confusion, when he confronted Mac standing in front of them spinning his car keys around his finger.

Madlin wiped his hand across his semi-conscious forehead. Mac threw him the keys and pointed to the Terraplane parked conveniently on the corner of the lot.

"Your driver shouldn't have parked on the street," Mac said, tossing the keys at one of the gang. "Take the Hudson. Take Outer Drive—fast, a few miles—then head west. They'll catch you if you try to go straight to The Loop."

Grinder Madlin's response started with the word *Mother*, but wasn't anything you'd repeat in front the family.

Four men headed for the Terraplane, and the other two made a run for the car in the street. The car in the street was moving even as they climbed on the running boards, just missing a stream of police cars speeding North down Sheridan. Dutch Webb's crew surrounded the Terraplane, fighting each other for a door. Once inside, the engine revved and they streaked down the road headed in the opposite direction.

Mac exhaled a heavy sigh, pulled out a pack of cigarettes and slipped one into his mouth. Then he remembered his date.

He'd have to make up an excuse for his missing hat and tie. He hoped Mara hadn't gotten too good of a look at the ones he'd been wearing earlier. The last thing he needed was a mob boss's cousin who knew he was The Bagman. Luckily, half the men at the hotel were wearing the same kind of navy suit he was.

He put the cigarette back in the pack and went back into the hotel the same way he'd come out, headed for the kitchen again. When he stuck his head back into the Marine Room the crowd seemed to be taking a collective sigh themselves. Medics helped the wounded while others shuffled around, talking to each other, checking their belongings and ordering drinks.

"They streaked down the road..."

He spotted Mara the same time she spotted him. She'd been speaking to an elderly couple, helping to calm some of their hysteria. Smiling, she put one arm around Mac and messed up his hair with her other hand.

"What happened to you?" she said.

"I'm not real big on armed robberies, or the parade of policemen that usually follow them." Mac tossed a few bills onto their table. "Why don't you and I get out of here?"

"Sounds good. We could always go for a nice evening ride, get some fresh air."

"Or a walk on the beach," Mac said. "I kind of had to loan the car to your brother."

"So that explains it," Mara said. She wrapped Mac's arm in hers and the two of them stepped outside. The weather was warm and breezy, not quite yet autumn. Shades of the crowd that had been in the hotel still gathered in batches on the beach. Mara stopped to take off her shoes before stepping into the sand. Mac didn't bother.

A hundred feet from the shoreline, she plopped down on the beach ignoring her wardrobe. Her legs sticking out from under her skirt in front of her, she glanced in both directions as she spoke, checking to make sure no one else was too close.

"That was him, wasn't it? My cousin's gang, I mean. They held up the hotel."

"Yeah, but I have to say, if they'd have planned it a little better it would've been a heck of a heist. Of course it doesn't help that Curtis Hatfield is crazy. You can't threaten people like that and still have them act fast."

"You know, Mr. McCullough, I think there may be more to you than you let on."

"Nah, I'm hopelessly shallow."

Mara laughed. Then there was a moment of silence. A light brightened in her eyes, and she stared at Mac curiously.

"What?" Mac said, still standing up and holding her hand.

"Come here a minute." She whispered, then pulled him down and kissed him on the lips. "That's for being a nice guy. Now, why don't we just forget the dancing and driving, and maybe go for a walk on the beach—see where we end up."

Where they ended up didn't matter. The two spent the night talking about their hopes and dreams, the past and the future. Mac kept his version deliberately vague. After stopping for one more drink, he asked Mara if she might be thinking of moving.

"I'll be fine," she said. "I've got a pack of relatives back home that'd kill Cousin Grinder if anything happened to me."

Mac kissed her goodnight at the door, before rejecting her invitation to come inside. He'd take the train home and pick up the Terraplane later. He had some things to do before he met with Grinder Madlin again.

●●●

Stepping off the El at the Addison Ravenswood stop, Mac remembered the totaled Model-A he'd left in Crankshaft's lot. If the "old man" had come back in to work at night as he often did, now wouldn't be the best time to talk to him. Turning in the other direction, he strolled a block down to the Lincoln Avenue Woolworth's. He ordered a soda at the fountain, and then went scanning the magazine rack where he found a copy of Dime Detective.

Leaving the five-and-dime, Mac strolled down the street and lit a cigarette. Stopping for the crossing signal, he was scanning the pages for the latest Race Williams adventure when the brick wall next to his head suddenly popped twice.

A clay splinter hit him in the cheek the same time he heard the shot. Somebody was still gunning for him.

Cursing, Mac rolled backward into an alley. He wiped the blood off his cheek and looked around only to find it was a dead-end. He needed high ground.

Moving at high speed, he grabbed a metal trashcan out of the corner and wedged the lid onto it, then set the can underneath the steps of a fire escape. In one motion he bunny-hopped on top of the trash can, leapt into the air and grabbed the bottom rung. Climbing the steps before the ladder slid to the ground, within moments he was up the fire escape and on the roof of a long, three-story, brick building. Behind the shadows of a factory's cylindrical chimney, McCullough unholstered his gun and began scanning the neighborhood.

The darkness seemed to hide everything under two stories that wasn't below a streetlight. There were still a few pedestrian stragglers on the street, some of them looking around to see which car had backfired. Nobody else was looking for a shooter. Then again, nobody else had been shot at. Mac remembered what Mirella the fortune teller had told him.

There is a butcher leading a horde of butchers...

He crouched, unmoving, watching. The late summer breeze fizzled to dead air. The streets and buildings around him were still. He waited, feeling for the Bagman's mask in his pocket. He still didn't have his hat. He would have liked to have thrown it into target range, just to see if somebody took a shot at it. But no, this was a game of patience. He made like a statue, everything but his eyes.

A blur of darkness shifted to his right. But that's not where the danger was. Because, even as the shadows shifted, an oily black form slid over the chimney directly above him.

Mac spun and something hit him on the head. He reeled forward and stuck out his hand to support himself. The lights almost went out, came back bright white then subsided to pinpoint. A sound he didn't recognize came out of his mouth as he battled for consciousness. But he refused to pass out. The pinpoint broadened to a hazy view that slipped in and out of focus.

"You forgot to give Grinder's boys your 'get out of my city' speech," a nasal, muffled voice hissed.

Something grabbed Mac by the cheek and shook his head violently.

"You are such a cream puff, aren't you, Mr. McCullough? I've been watching you, though. You got a nice racket, but you honestly have no idea how small time you are. Even with that mask on, you're still just a con man and a cat burglar."

The raspy voice grated at Mac's ears. Before he'd realized it, he grabbed his tormentor's wrist in an effort to throw him off balance. Something hit him again, hard, directly on top of the head.

The white lights exploded.

Mac was suddenly aware of something slapping the side of his face. He'd lost consciousness.

"Wake up! Wake up, you maggot! Don't you pass out on me! Don't you dare! No, no, no, no, no, no, no, you don't get to pass out. You have to watch it all. You and I are going to have *so much* fun."

Mac reached for his gun. It wasn't there. Something grabbed him by the hair and started shaking his head.

"My city! Mine! You hear me!" The voice rattled and spat the harder Mac's head shook. Then it stopped, wheezing, as if to collect itself. "You seem to understand things just fine in your Mac McCullough persona, but *you* need to understand that your masked friend is only going to get you killed. You want make a little extra graft, fine—but *do not* mess with the Butcher Shop! I will unload an entire horde on you. I know who you are. I know who your friends are. If I ever see that mask again... Well, you might just wish you had stayed in that little cigar store of yours selling candy to the little kiddies."

The white light parted and Mac saw a light gray silhouette, a gray flat cap and a long coat. Something punched him right on the vertebrae at the bottom of his neck and a stinging shock darted through every nerve ending in his body.

"I am the boss. The Butcher. Do *not* mess with the Butcher Shop!"

Mac never saw what hit him. The white light parted, and he fell into a black hole.

●●●

The rain almost woke Mac up. At first he couldn't move his body. He lay there face down on the roof and stared sideways for a while. It took every bit of his will to roll over on his back before the rain hitting him in the face truly began to rouse him.

"Den what ya shooting at me for?" he mumbled, still mentally in the fight. He sat up, only to become aware of his throbbing head. Except it wasn't just his head, it was his whole body. Whatever that last punch was, it had messed him up. He could feel every nerve ending, every bruised muscle throb. His stomach turned over. A sweat broke out beneath his clothes.

Crawling back toward the chimney, Mac climbed up the side. He took three steps toward the fire escape and fell down again. A few minutes later a black-gray blob slid over the building's parapet like a wet rat climbing over a fence.

The fire escape made a crashing sound as Mac bounced down the ladder and hit the first landing on his back. Cussing, he reached for the handrail and pulled himself up awkwardly. The light wavered and he almost passed out again. Using the handrail for support he slowly made his way down. On the last level he sat on the steps, letting his weight work for him as it lowered the stairs to the ground.

He slid sideways down the alley leaning against the wall for support. Staggering down the sidewalk like a drunk, he paused every once in a while to lean against a tree, a fence, anything that would support him on his way down the street. Slowly, he made his way underneath the El tracks. Still leaning on the rickety fence for support, he made his way down the alley until he grasped the gate to Crankshaft's Auto Repair.

It took him ten minutes to pick the same lock he'd cracked in two minutes earlier. The game he and Crankshaft played with the locks didn't seem so funny now. He stumbled for Crankshaft's shack, just to the side of the rickety sheet-metal garage where the ace mechanic parked the cars he was working on.

Mac couldn't even pick that lock. Instead, he stumbled for the Bagman's underground garage on back of the lot. He tripped and rolled into one of the piles of junk that camouflaged the entry to the underground lair. Sliding down the side of the pile he made a seat for himself and collapsed using the junk for a backrest.

●●●

Crankshaft didn't find him until the next morning. Carrying the big man to the underground garage, he then cleaned and bandaged his wounds. He laid Mac in the cot they kept there for just such occasions. Then switched off the ceiling light and went back upstairs to work in the sun.

Mac's barely conscious mind knew he must have looked bad off. Crankshaft hadn't even mentioned the Model-A he'd totaled.

•••

"This stinks, Crank. I don't know how much longer I can hold out."

"Gotten addicted to that mask, haven't you?"

Two weeks had passed, and Mac had refused to make an appearance as The Bagman since he'd been beaten up by the mysterious Butcher. Bad enough the killer knew where Mac lived, but even worse, the Butcher knew where all Mac's friends and adopted family were. He was a threat to them all. As far as Mac knew, every move he made was being watched.

He'd kept sleeping at his apartment, even with the lingering threat of sudden violence, because if he'd moved they'd know that too. The few hiding places he had left, he saved.

He'd continued to roust barrooms for Grinder Webb and no more threats had been made. At least now he knew who—or what—Grinder was working for. He'd also taken Mara out on a few dates since then and been glad to realize that wasn't why the Butcher had shot at him.

What he did know was this. If the Butcher hadn't killed him, he must have a use for him. And Mac didn't like to be used. For the past two weeks he'd been banging his head on the wall trying to come up with a plan. He had nothing. He was bluffing, and he still had to wait for the stakes to be raised.

Meanwhile, the Butcher's mob had finally riled up Frank Nitti's Outfit. Tommy guns were back in style, along with bombs, bullets, and the bodies of innocent bystanders. Three men in a Lincoln killed on Western Ave— Nitti's gang. Four men in a sedan on Halsted—Grinder or the Butcher's. And wherever both gangs met, they left a trail of dead and wounded behind them. The gangs wouldn't have bothered Mac so much, but the stray bullets didn't care who they hit. The death of innocents made him angry, and the daily toll spiraled into the dozens.

It had been lucky for Mac he was just a "salesman," but now Nitti had armed men on the lookout just like Grinder. Both sides were looking for a fight. The stakes were already high. Mac knew the next bar he rousted could be his last.

"So, what are you going to do?" Crankshaft said.

"I don't know. I've been trying to come up with something. This waiting is killing me."

"Well, I want to applaud your patience. I know that's not normal for you. You must be learning— something."

"No, not really." Mac glanced up from the floor he'd been staring at and

forced an unconvincing smile onto his face. While he had told the ace mechanic about the loss of The Bagman's secret identity, he had neglected
to tell him the part about The Bagman's friends. Mac figured if they were
going to get murdered, he didn't want them spending their last hours wor-
rying about it. He had to do something.

Yet the more he thought about it, he had to wait. There was some reason
the Butcher had kept him alive. So at some point, they'd either up the ante
or kill him. He had to wait and find out what they upped the ante with. He
knew in a blackmail game like this it was risky as hell. The Butcher's Shop
owned everything about this operation. They could herd him where they
wanted to, they could take hostages, they could pull a frame-up, and, they'd
kill Mac's friends if he did anything before they sprung their big surprise.

But surprises were Mac's specialty—or at least they used to be. He just
had to be there to throw a wrench in works.

"You ever hear back from Kerr and Tobar?" Crankshaft said. He was
straightening the office and getting ready to lock up.

"The 'Katchandhammer Kids?' Let me tell you, Crank, those boys are
every bit chock-full-o'-weird as Mirella. You see 'em, tell them I'm looking
for 'em. I don't even know how to reach the two. They just show up."

"Kind of like Mirella."

"Don't get me started on that King of Thieves stuff, Crank. I'm looking around, but these guys got nothing to steal. The one thing I know is
that everything they've got is stashed at that armory they call the Purity
Meat Plant, Back O' the Yards. The Federal Treasury by the Stock Exchange
would be easier to break into. At least they wouldn't have as many guns."
Mac took off his hat and felt the knot on his head. He wedged the hat back
on, deciding to keep it there for padding.

"I've even looked at it like a bank job," he said. "Except these slaughterhouse guys are never open, so you can't case the joint. And even when
I have been in the building, the guards won't let you into the other half.
The place is surrounded by a hundred square yards of nothing, and even
if I could tunnel in, I wouldn't know where to tunnel to. And even if I did
know, it's probably in an iron safe I don't know the make of, surrounded
by two feet of concrete block. This stinks. The first rule of a good premedi-
tated crime is to case the joint, and I'm not even sure the joint is the joint,
and if it is the joint, then where in the joint is it?"

"Well, whatever you do, just remember I told you not to, OK?" Crankshaft said. He pulled a bottle of bootleg corn liquor out of his desk and
began to pour them both a drink.

"Thanks, Crank, but just one." Mac looked at his watch. "I've got a date."

"Nice to see you finally go out with a normal girl."

"Her cousin's a mobster."

"For you, that's normal. Funny though, you always struck me as more of a Dime Western guy than a Ranch Romance man."

"The Masked Rider," Mac said. The two desperadoes toasted, and he thought about the risk he'd put his friends' lives in. He felt like a rat.

●●●

"So, how's your cousin Jake doing?" Mac asked. He wiped the orange sauce off the side of his mouth and dropped the napkin back in his lap.

"Meaner than ever," Mara said, manipulating her chopsticks like they were part of her hand and dropping a clump of noodles into her mouth.

Mac had borrowed Crankshaft's Chevy Universal AD again and managed to pick up Mara without letting Grinder know he'd been there. He'd agreed to chop-suey at a Chinese restaurant for dinner, but only if they could go see *The Eagle and the Hawk* at the movie theater afterward—knowing full well it would be no problem since Mara had a crush on Cary Grant.

"I'm worried his job's in danger though," she said, in between bites.

Mac didn't bother to mention that in Grinder's line of work, if your job was in danger so was your life. The day after the mix up at the Edgewater Hotel, Grinder had returned from a "secret" meeting even more beaten up than he had been after the heist. He'd been confined to bed for two days, and it had taken a week for his walk to finally return to normal. Mac figured the Butcher had probably beaten his inner-ear out.

"Can I ask you a question?" Mac put down his silverware and waited, staring into her eyes. "Are you happy? I mean, are you really happy living in a house full of mobsters, holding down a full-time job, and then coming home and cleaning up after all those bozos?"

"I don't really have to clean up after any of them, Mac. They're never there. And the mobster thing keeps me on my toes. I don't break the law, but I can understand people who do. These are hard times."

"And they create hard people. Those people, they hurt others without caring, and, they hurt all of us without even knowing it."

"Ooooooo, there it is!" Mara pointed at him with her chopsticks. "That mysterious, dark Mac McCullough again. Where did he come from? You needn't worry about me, Mac. Is there something bothering you?"

Mac hadn't told Mara about the Bagman, and he certainly hadn't told her that her life might be in danger, but it didn't take a psychiatrist to see he'd been looking over his shoulder for the past two weeks.

"So you are happy with where you are?" Mac said. "I mean, could you go the rest of your life this way?"

"Working in a packing plant? I don't think I could do that for the rest of my life, but yes, I'm quite happy. I'm happy with you. Now, why so jumpy?"

"This mob your cousin works for, they call themselves the Butcher Shop. It's obvious they're from out of town. They weren't around here in the twenties, when half the city was killing each other. It not only kills people, but it scars the ones left alive. Folks are forced to change, and when they're forced—most of the time, their humanity fades. The animal side wins out." He realized he was about to start talking about himself, and made sure not to. "And those two sides—animal and human—they're just like the mobs, neither side ever gives up. It's a war the civilians have to carry around with them every day."

"You know that much sympathy can be harmful. You start making up stories in your head."

"Yeah, well, you weren't around here in the twenties."

Mac neglected to mention that for half that time he hadn't been either. After his father had been murdered, Mac McCullough had left Chicago. For ten years he'd hopped trains and grifted from heist to heist, all the while learning. Only when he returned to Chicago, he found himself using the criminal's own methods against them. He'd gone from committing crimes to committing criminals. An unstable position at best, since he was one. Now, he'd found himself heir to the Gypsy legend of The King of Thieves, which, as far as instability goes, was like living in a house constructed of tight wires and see-saws.

"The whole city changed back then," he said, without mentioning how much he had. "Everybody was paid off. Justice was a bribe. You don't give people an even break, they'll start busting heads to break even. The people on the bottom, good people that did everything right, are the ones that pay the price."

"You do know they already voted to repeal Prohibition. This can't go on much longer."

"Yeah, I know," Mac said. "I need to wait. Be patient." He was almost speaking to himself.

"But not too patient," Mara said. "We've only got a few minutes for the fortune cookies before the picture starts."

The waiter arrived with the check and the fortune cookies. Mac handed the waiter a five and they cracked the strips of paper out of the cookies like eggs from a shell. Mara unwound the tiny scroll. She laughed before she read it out loud.

"You will meet a dark and mysterious man." She pointed at Mac and laughed again.

Mac had yet to notice. He'd only glanced at his fortune and was still staring blankly at the words on it.

Sometimes the animal must win to preserve the species of man.
--Mirella

"What's yours say, Mac?" Mara tried to snatch the tiny piece of paper from his hand.

Mac tore Mirella's name off the strip of paper and handed it across the table.

"Sometimes the animal must win to..." She glanced back up at Mac. "Weird, weren't you just talking about something like that? What do you suppose it means?"

"Mankind is his own worst enemy." There was an uncomfortable moment of silence as Mac stared into space.

"And to defeat that enemy, what do we need?" Mara stood up like a cheerleader and grabbed him by the arm. "That's right, cowboy! *The Eagle and the Hawk*! And if Cary Grant can't save humanity, who can?"

"Carole Lombard?" Mac said. Lombard was the film's leading lady.

"Lombard *and* the Keystone Cops!" Mara said, dragging Mac toward the door.

It took him a few minutes to stop glancing over the edges of rooftops for snipers before he calmed down a little. A cool breeze blew down the windy corridors from the lake as they sauntered down Southport to the Music Box Theater where the show was playing. Boys were playing stickball off a side alley. A small flock of children ran beside the curb chasing a barrel hoop as it rolled toward Mac and Mara from up the street. Three men in suits crossed the sidewalk in front of them and climbed into a car.

"Hey, I see you finally got rid of that ugly yellow tie," Mara said, stepping back as the barrel hoop crashed into the wall to their left.

Mac stopped in his tracks as a young boy and girl chased each other into the open door of a funeral home. Putting his arm around Mara, the young couple began stepping in unison again.

"Yeah, much as I love that tie, I had to—"

Without warning, the doorway behind them exploded. Mac felt the shockwave beneath his feet before he turned back to see a plume of smoke jet out the funeral home door and into the street. The little girl that had just run inside lay unconscious by the sidewalk. The boy was nowhere in sight. Mac sprinted to the girl and put his hand on her neck, feeling for her pulse. There was none.

Bounding back to the door, he stepped inside and saw the puddle of blood and flesh that had been the other child. Inside the funeral home an entire back wall had been blown open to reveal the speakeasy that was hidden there. Mac had known there was a speakeasy in back, but he had completely forgotten about it. Through the smoke, he could see people lying on the floor and against the walls, wounded and dying, screaming for help.

The crowd outside was too frightened to rush into the building like Mac had. Surrounded by the smoke inside the doorway, the big man reached into his pocket for a pair of gloves and the mask that made him both a hero and a criminal.

Outside the door, a cloud of smoke rolled over the sidewalk and onto the street. The Bagman stepped out of it like the demon he was accused of being.

Glancing over his shoulder, he saw Mara kneeling over the little girl with no pulse, still trying to revive her. Without thought, he turned toward the street.

Those three men he'd seen coming out of the funeral home. Nobody gets that lucky.

He glanced over even as their cruiser was pulling into the street. The driver's head pivoted nervously in every direction, obviously worried about a lot more than oncoming traffic. Curtains were pulled across the rear windows so the men in back couldn't be seen.

Unfortunately for them, that meant they couldn't see what was coming.

When the car shifted into first the King of Thieves stood on the rear bumper. He'd barely gotten his grip on the rear panel as the car slung west for a few blocks, then south, headed for the Back o' the Yards. Mac remembered his date for a second. He didn't have time for this.

Then he heard the voice of Curtis "The Cleaver" Hatfield speak, and the men in the car laughing in response. He remembered the fortune Mirella had written. *Sometimes the animal must win...*

Launching himself with his legs, The Bagman slid over the cruiser's trunk and gripped the edge of the rear window without making a sound. Gripping with one hand as the car took a tight corner, he yanked the .45 out of his shoulder holster.

Back on the straightaway, the Criminal Detective fired four rounds into the car's back seat. Two different screams emanated from inside the car, followed by a collection of curses and prayers. Glass shot like shrapnel as gunfire burst from multiple barrels out the back window. Still in high gear, the automobile slowed and jerked, waiting for the driver to downshift. There was a brief silence as he pressed on the clutch as if all the noise had collapsed in on itself.

One of the gangsters inside threw the rear curtain open and fired from the backseat, but no one was there. The men on either side of him sat huddled in the corners, clutching their wounds. One with his hands on his head, the other on his stomach. The car lurched then began to speed up again.

"What the hell is it?" Hatfield screamed.

"Idunno. Theygotguns!"

Hatfield stuck his head out the window looking for gang members from Nitti's forces. No one was even behind them.

"Where'd they go!" Hatfield wasn't asking, he was ordering. His men replied in rapid fire sentences that made no sense. As they pulled to a stop near Ashland Avenue, Hatfield screamed. "Where the hell are they! Who the hell are they!"

The only other conscious man in the car remained silent.

Without warning, the ceiling of the cab exploded and two shots ripped into Hatfield's shoulders. The car began to veer across the opposite lane, narrowly missing an oncoming Ford. A mysterious masked figure launched itself from the roof of the car as the gangster's getaway veered hard into a ditch and rolled. The masked man landed on the other side of the ditch in the grass. He dropped and rolled just like the car, but came up standing on his feet and shoving fresh bullets into his revolver.

The car lay upside down, rocking back and forth, springs squeaking and steam erupting from under the hood.

Horns began honking and traffic began to shift again, except for a few heroic drivers pulling over to see if they could help. Mac stood tall in the shadows, blending in with the ivy draped next to a brick wall with his gun at his side. Nothing in the car moved.

The crowd began to shift and mix with the smoke from the wreckage. The drivers coming to the rescue were getting too close. He'd be seen. And even if he did manage to avoid their detection, the police would be there any second.

And Mac had a date.

He slapped himself in the head and rolled backward into the bushes. Taking off his mask as he came out the other side, Mac found himself standing in a gas station parking lot. It was only a couple of blocks down Grace Street back to where the chase had started. If he ran as fast as he could, he might be able to get back in time for Mara not to notice he'd been missing. Or at least in time to make up an explanation.

He had just cut the corner through somebody's yard on Ashland and Grace, when something hit him in back of the head. Everything went wavy, and Mac fell to his knees. He could feel the grass on his hands. Something hit him again.

He wondered what the grass would feel like on his face, but he didn't remember clenching his teeth or falling face first into it. He remembered his date and a vacuum tube buzzed in his head. Then it popped and everything went out.

•••

Mac lay there with his eyes fluttering for a while before he remembered anything. Everything was black. He blinked his eyes some more, but it stayed that way. His hand reached for his head and he realized his mask was on sideways. He straightened it, but the darkness remained. He waited. Staring into space, he became aware of a faint circle of light hundreds of feet above him. He waited some more, hoping his vision would adjust to the dark. It didn't.

Moving his head, the circle of brightness came into better view. Like cheap neon lighting a mile away, it almost cast a shadow on the rusty iron bars above him. He hoped it was mud he lay in, then rolled over and passed out again.

Later, something nibbled at his ankle and he jumped to his feet. The darkness hung like a curtain, and he waited, praying for more light. He felt for a match in his pockets, but whoever had knocked him out had emptied them. They'd even taken his belt. He could hear water flowing in the background like an underground stream or a sewer.

It took him a while, but he could tell he was below the streets, somewhere in the nest of drainage sewers beneath the city. He grappled the bars above his head and shook them, but nothing stirred, not even the dust. They were easily an inch thick and manufactured to last ages.

Unable to see the walls where he was imprisoned, Mac gingerly began to feel about his dank, dark cell. Judging from the faint circle of light he was at least a hundred yards underground, locked in some sort of concrete block, something like a curbside concrete drain with a length of iron bars locked across the top. For a moment he thought he could hear Lake Michigan's waves breaking on the rocks in the background.

He felt something bite his ankle. Mac kicked at it in reflex and something squealed. Glancing down at the floor, Mac found himself staring at a horde of verminous yellow eyes reflecting cold, ravenous hunger.

Rats. A tiny pack of them swirled in the mud and grime that filled the bottom of the concrete block cage.

Mac reached for his gun, but remembered his entire shoulder rig had been confiscated the moment he touched his chest. He felt the pockets of his coat, vest, and then his slacks, again. He'd been completely cleaned out.

One of the rats nipped at Mac's pants leg again, and the big man kicked it away, stomping. Something nipped at his other heel and he realized he'd just picked a fight with a gang. He gripped the thick iron rungs above him.

Using them to hold himself upright, the big man stomped all over the bottom of the pit. Squeals, thrashing, and gnashing teeth spat mud, blood and muck all over Mac's flailing calves. Till the only sound in the chamber, a tiny squeak, exhaled and faded into the hiss of a flat bicycle tire.

Mac stood with every muscle in his body tensed, gasping, still grasping the iron bars. Shifting his feet, he realized the bottom of the cage was now filled with blood, fur, and bones, as well as the original mud. It looked like he wouldn't be sitting down too soon.

The iron grate over his concrete bunker was state made, probably to keep bigger varmints out. Pulling his head up to the grating, he still couldn't see where he was. He put both feet on one of the walls and flexed, trying to bend one of the iron bars, but it was impossible. Mac lowered himself to the ground and scanned the bottom again. What he couldn't see with his eyes, he felt out with his hands.

So much mold and grime covered the walls it took him a few minutes to feel a tiny hole in the concrete wall to his left, about two feet from the bottom of the cage. That had to be where the rats had crawled in.

Sifting through the corners with the toes of his shoes he heard something clink. Feeling around on the floor, he found part of a broken bottle. It was almost green, but once he'd wiped the mud off of it he could see a little bit of a reflection. He stuck the piece of glass through the bars, trying to hold it so he could see its reflection and find out where he was. He had to lean against the wall to get the angle just right, but he could just make out a sort of a street running above him. Except he wasn't on a street, he was in some kind of sewer drainage area where all the city's pipes fed into one another, some sort of giant channel. An industrial sluice.

Rain had been forecast for the evening. Mac gazed at the blackness above and realized he only had a few hours at most.

A row of iron barred gutters ran down the "street" on either side of him. Some were opened, but most were locked. That's when he realized it wasn't just the sewer he had smelled.

He'd thought it was the mold and mildew of the drainage left in the concrete cells, but now that he'd taken a second whiff he recognized it for what it was. Death, the unmistakable smell of rotting flesh. Some of the trash stuck on the grating above him resembled shreds of another man's suit. He looked down at his feet and thought he was going to throw up for a second.

Mac screamed for help. It was the middle of the day, but nobody noticed. He yelled for an hour or two, then leaned with his back against the wall and crossed his arms. Help was not coming.

Given the fact that this sluice was some sort of industrial set-up, all his captors had to do to kill him was wait for a heavy rain. Or they could just leave him here to rot. The bars were unbreakable and he couldn't reach the lock.

"His captors?" he chided himself. There was only one. The Butcher.

A rat plopped through the hole in the wall and fell at his feet. Mac looked for something to plug the hole with and wound up shoving a few handfuls of muck into it, then smoothing it with the back of his hand. He could sense something moving in the pipe, but he didn't hear any more squeaking.

He spent most of the afternoon scraping the sides of his prison looking for cracks in the concrete, a flaw in one of the iron bars, or some tool he could use to escape. All he came up with was another sliver of glass and some pebbles.

He waited until after school let out, in hopes some kids playing where they shouldn't be might find him. Then he yelled some more. The only response was the sound of a thundercloud. He estimated the sun was setting outside. Things were only going to get darker. If he didn't drown, he'd starve, or get eaten by rats.

He sat there in the black awhile and listened to his stomach eat itself. For lack of anything better to do, he went through his pockets again. He searched every crack of the tiny four-by-two cell one more time, and all he could see were the bars. If the sluice filled he could drown any minute.

Like a rat.

That's when it struck him. The cage next to his was open! The rats had no tools and they had no problem tunneling from cage to cage. Mac chewed on the inside of his jaw, and remembered they had lots of pointy, sharp teeth. He still needed a tool.

He had searched himself and the cell three times and come up with nothing. Rocks and glass, that was all. He was about to punch the wall when he thought of his shoes. His *steel toed* shoes.

The only honest work Mac had ever done in his life had been in construction. Even while fighting crime and pretending to run a cigar store, he had kept dabbling in small neighborhood building jobs. He'd originally bought the steel toed brogues for those unscheduled visits to the construction site, but when he'd starting fighting with the mob he'd found them irreplaceable. Now, he was hoping they would save his life. He wasn't sure how, but maybe, just maybe, he might be able to dig out, or wedge the grate open, or even pick the lock, but it all depended on the material of his shoes.

Thunder echoed in the background, and a chorus of dripping water slapped the concrete with a hard, high pitched rhythm. He could hear the sound of a stream somewhere coming for him.

He took off his shoe and began scraping the side of it on the concrete by the bars above. He peeled the shine and several layers of leather off with the first few swipes, revealing the steel toe, but realized he had to find a way to pull the sole off the shoe. Luckily, they were crepe gumshoes.

"He sat there in the black awhile…"

The rain came. Cold water bit his ankles as it slowly began filling the bottom of his cell. Mac pulled the piece of glass he'd used to look at his surroundings earlier out of his pocket and began to tear at the stitches along the edge of the shoe sole.

The water continued to rise. Mac heard some of his rat friends chirping in the background. The water rose above his knee level and continued to rise. Even if he could tear apart his shoe in time, what was he going to do with it? Dig his way out? There was no time. A tiny ocean waved awash around him. The water was rising too fast.

Mac tore the sole off his shoe. He freed the steel toe from its binding and put it in his pocket with the sliver of glass. At the back of the heel, he found a strip of metal reinforcing the heel. He peeled that off, along with every nail, stitch, or reinforcement he could find, before sticking the scraps of the leather uppers in his back pocket.

Cold water rose to the level of his thigh. Mac bit down on the strip of metal a few times, and began feeling around outside the bars for the lock that held the grate down. He couldn't reach it. If he could, it probably would have been filled with muck, or the Butcher may have just broken the original key off in there.

"King of Thieves, my freezing ass. Knight of cups—yeah, right." Mac said between shivers, and curled his arms around himself. Convinced the Fates hated him, he cursed them. "Hey, Mirella, according to your stupid legend, I'm supposed to have this amazing luck. Well, where the hell is it? Because from where I'm standing all that 'what's-been-written' stuff is only going to get my ass kicked."

Mac listened to the sound of the water rushing into the drains around him.

"Or killed," he thought. The air was full of mist now. He could hear the rains steady beat as the water approached waist level—No, it was already up to his belly.

He was going to drown.

Mac felt down in the water for the tiny hole in the wall, as if somehow getting his hand into it might free him. It didn't.

Pulling the piece of glass out of his pocket, Mac held it above the bars to look at the reflection one more time. Even before he saw it, he could hear the water's rush increasing. Above him, in the "gutter" he was locked underneath, the concrete sluice flowed like rapids in the rainy season. Something clunked and a wave roared in the background. The water rose higher and began to flow over the bars into Mac's tiny bunker. He lowered his head as a sudden wave drenched him. Water poured through the bars in buckets.

Sticking the reflective glass back in his pocket, he grabbed onto the iron bars with the steely grip of a man holding on for his life. He hung his head low as the water slopped in from above. The hole in the side of the cell was below water level now, but a steady stream still flowed in, menacing him both from above and below.

With the rain above, the blackness closed in. The water rose to his chest, then his neck. A chill ran up the back of his head as the cold hit his collar. No longer able to lower his head without drowning, he held it up and closed his eyes, still clasping the iron bars with fingers like steel cables.

He pulled himself up, sticking his face between the bars and gasped for breath between the waves. The flow of water steadied, but it was up to Mac's nose now. And, he had another stream above him about to overflow into his cell. The iron bars pressed on his face. One of his arms flailed toward the lock, but he still couldn't reach it. He held on in the dark, his hands and nose the only things above the water.

He never saw the wave that engulfed him.

●●●

Mac shivered, but he wasn't conscious. His hands were raw, and his head felt like he'd swallowed a fish tank. He opened his eyes and remembered where he was again. Something lodged in the top of his lungs. He sat up, coughing up water and bile on himself before he scraped his way to the wall and laid his back against it.

His eyes had either adjusted to the dark, or the rain had stopped and it was brighter in the world above. Glancing across the floor, he stared at his shoeless foot for a moment, then pulled the soggy sock off, and slapped it on the damp concrete. His feet were pruned, waterlogged and wrinkly. The rest of his body, too.

How long had he been out? He had no idea. It could have been hours, it could have been days. All the moments mixed into one black vision. Time had stopped.

He sat there staring like a zombie, but even with his eyes adjusted to the dark everything was black. With the occasional sound of sewage dripping from the world above, the open silence between the beats swallowed him. He closed his eyes and exhaled, his spirit deflated.

Something squeaked next to his right ear. Mac jumped reflexively and skittered to his left. The damned rats were climbing back in the cell again. If he didn't drown, or starve, he'd be eaten.

Mac swept a hand in the direction he heard the squeak come from. His hand skimmed the face of his rodent cell mate. He could feel the rat's whiskers slipping between his fingers. Still, he'd caught something in the palm of his hand.

He stood up and held the tiny piece of rock above the bars of his cell, trying to see what it was in the dim light above, still not knowing if it was day or night. Turning the chip of stone over in his fingers, he determined it was a tiny sliver of concrete. The rats *were eating* their way in.

For the first time in a day, Mac McCullough almost smiled. Reaching into his pocket, he removed the steel toe from his shoes, got down on one knee and began to dig around the rat hole. The concrete on the edges seemed to crumble a little, and then a little more with each tiny scrape.

"Thank God for substandard construction materials," Mac muttered. He had never thought of a racketeer's negligence saving his life before. He could feel more dust in the air with every scrape, but the concrete spilled out of the hole in pebbles and silt. It was like shoveling a spoonful at a time, but whenever he stopped to rest, he got bored and started digging again. There was nothing else to do.

Thunder echoed from above, and he began to dig faster as he thought of the water running over his head again. It was like a race where everybody else already had a head start. While the rest of the world was sprinting, The Bagman ran a marathon in one place. He kept his movement constant, his pace steady. It took four hours before he could fit his arm into the hole.

He wadded up his jacket and stuck it under his arm, so it wouldn't rub against the concrete, and continued to scrape the inside of the hole-turned-tunnel in long, straight motions. Then after a while, he scraped the rest of the detritus out of the hole and began scraping again. Six hours later he had a hole about a foot wide on his side and two feet deep.

By late afternoon, he had torn a good deal of the flesh around his finger-nails away. He couldn't see them and he tried not to think about it. After an hour or so, he would change hands and start the whole process over again. A while longer and he thought he could see the glowing yellow eyes of another pack of rats, but Mac was working by rote now, almost as if in trance. The only thing in his mind was escape, the digging, and the next breath. He saw the ravenous yellow eyes, but the thought of them never entered his head. They were not part of the plan.

He knew they were more scared of him than he was of them. He rapped the side of the tunnel with the shoe's steel toe every few minutes, and the eyes would disappear. If he lost consciousness again he'd be lunch.

Just thinking about it, Mac cuffed himself in the face to stay awake then continued to scrape the inside of the hole, slapping the side of it with the steel toe and shoveling more concrete out, one tablespoon at a time. Scrape, slap, shovel. Scrape, slap, shovel.

A few hours later he realized there was a small pile of concrete gravel in his cell. He dug with his entire shoulder shoved into the wall now. He was weak. He had a headache. He was tired, hungry, and getting thirsty. He couldn't very well suck the sewer water out of the mud in the corner of his cell and drink it, so if it rained he'd drown, and if it didn't he'd die of thirst.

And after that, thought ceased. There was only one way out. Scrape, slap, shovel. Scrape, slap, shovel.

The biggest problem was the size of Mac's shoulders and his barrel chest. An ordinary man might have been able to squeeze his way through a hole a square foot wide, but even with gymnastic abilities bordering on the supernatural, Mac still needed at least a few more inches.

His head felt light. White light.

If he passed out he'd be food for the rats.

He dug in, down, hard, and fast for two minutes, and couldn't take it anymore. Without thinking, he thrust one arm and his head into the tiny tunnel. Bending his neck, shoulders and spine, he groped, pulling himself ahead with one hand, pushing with his legs. His fingers felt raw, his skin felt prickly. His shoulders stuck.

But the same moment his hand felt the inside of the opposite wall. He gripped it as best as he could, and pulled until his head was at the far side of the tunnel, one arm extended into the next cell. Pressing the palm of his hand against the wall, Mac heaved. At first he just moved a little. Then he pressed at the wall behind him with his feet, pulling with one arm and all his might.

Concrete cracked off the wall like cheap plaster as Mac's right shoulder burst through the wall just above it. In one motion he popped into the next room up to his thighs, and then fell on his back onto the floor.

Part of him wanted to lie down and rest. He closed his eyed and started to sigh, then stopped halfway through. With a sudden jerk, Mac was back on his feet and swaying at the hips with his dukes up.

That moment he'd closed his eyes, he'd remembered the rats.

His head hit his chest and he shuddered, sinking, but when he reached up to grab the bars to support himself there was nothing there.

He would have shaken his head, if it didn't hurt so much. He lifted it instead. A thin ring of light hung some hundred feet above him, and there were no bars blocking his way. Mac shook his shoulder to get the blood flowing through his chest again. He stepped back, took a deep breath, then leaped, taking one step against and up the wall. With that he had both arms over the top of the gutter. He cursed. He still couldn't see where he was. He had a vision of himself crawling into a deeper hole.

An almost evil laughter echoed through the sewers as Mac hoisted one leg over the bunker's edge and rolled out onto the ledge above. Forcing himself to get up immediately, his feet slid over the algae covered concrete and he toppled to one knee, tearing the leg of his suit. He cursed some more and looked up at the barely burning ring of fire above.

Mac's eyes almost glowed in the dark. Groping, he felt his way across a small square stream and pressed his hand against the wall. Remembering the angle from both of his concrete cells, he put his back to the wall and groped his way in the direction of what he remembered to be the light. His right hand hit one of the ladder's metal rungs and his heart jumped.

Feeling those rusty rungs in both his hands, he hoped he had the strength to climb out. He sure as hell didn't consider hanging around. Some strange reflex made him check his pocket for his mask then he began to climb.

Once he got started it was a breeze, one step at a time. He climbed like an automaton and was reaching for another rung when his hand hit the manhole cover. With the top of his head pressed against the thick iron disk, Mac gripped the ladder with one hand and pushed the lid off with the other. It turned sideways in the slot, spun like a coin and almost hit him in the jaw. There was that weird laughter again, and then he shoved fifty pounds of state-wrought iron into the street.

The light blinded him and the fresh air made him dizzy. So much so, that Mac hurled himself out of the sewers and onto the surface for fear of falling back down the manhole. Sliding the lid back over it, he saw only blackness below.

He climbed to his feet to find himself standing on a paved, almost vacant lot next to Lake Michigan. At least it had been paved at one time, but now most of the concrete lie in chunks and piles of slivered asphalt—Mac's lucky substandard construction materials. The only sign of life was a couple of yachts up on blocks, being stored for the winter, and a rowboat. He had to close his eyes because of the brightness.

The fact that he was in a yacht storage facility told him he was somewhere around Goose Island where mariners stored their boats for winter. All he had to do now was get home.

He opened the slits of his eyes and looked down at himself. His jacket was gone and so was his wallet. His shirt was covered in mud, rust, and filth. A pant leg was missing and he had only one shoe. But he was alive. He had escaped.

"I'll walk home," he thought with a positive smile. "Anywhere is within walking distance if you have the time."

He inhaled deep, took a step, and then collapsed on the ground like a sack of overripe fruit. Then, on the brink of unconsciousness, the big man placed his hands under his head, rolled over on his side and proceeded to snore.

●●●

Mac woke up to the chills, and a man in painter's clothes kicking the bottom of his one-shoed foot. The man took off his hat and slung it to his side like he was about start slapping Mac with it.

"What are you doing sleeping on my site?"

"Knock it off already!" Mac held his arm over his eyes, the light still hurt them. Conscious of where he was, he realized the man in construction clothes must be working on the boats, and was most likely the foreman. "I'm no squatter buddy!"

The man in the painter's clothes lowered an eyebrow.

"And I'm not a drunk, either," Mac said, standing up and looking at himself. He pointed at the manhole cover. "Somebody knocked me out and locked me up in one of the gutters down there. Tried to drown me."

Mac was too tired to talk anymore. He put a hand on the construction worker's chest and gently shoved him out of the way. The man raised a fist, and, looking at Mac's face again, lowered it. Instead, the foreman placed his hands on his hips and watched the strange man in rags trudge through the gate until the figure reached the crossroads at the next intersection.

Mac hopped on back of a trolley car going toward the Loop. He got kicked off for not paying. He hopped another trolley and got kicked off for the way he looked. Then he hopped another one. He was past communicating, past asking for spare change. He had only one conscious thought. He had to get home. The trolleys were the way to go.

Hopping off at Ashland and Addison, he leaned forward to force his step and headed the half-block to his apartment. He'd been staring at the sidewalk ten feet in front of him the entire way, when he finally glanced up to take a look at his corner apartment.

It wasn't there.

Somebody had set his apartment on fire. Again.

He'd just moved a month ago, when a gangster had burned his house down, and now he was going to have to move again. Looking at the hole in the structure that had been his apartment house, he realized at least he didn't have anything to move.

And, most of his money had been hidden in the floorboards there.

The apartment was gone. The entire side of the building where his room was located had been burned up and gutted. It looked like an explosion had taken place. The floor of Mac's bathroom hung over the edge of where his room had been. The walls had been blown out, most likely by somebody leaving the gas on. Mac noticed the vacant apartments next to his. People had died here.

He really did need to find a place of his own.

Barely conscious, he already felt like he was watching a movie. His head faltered and he almost fell over. Then he turned left. Every step seemed to jar his bones, but he just kept going.

Beneath the shadows of the El tracks at the intersection of Addison and Damen is a little alley behind a hot dog stand. At the end of the alley sat a sign that read "Crankshaft's Car Repair and Sales." The shadows welcomed him.

Being morning, Crankshaft's gate was opened. A healthy Mac Mc-Cullough would have walked downstairs to the underground garage and simply lain on the cot until his strength recovered. But Mac didn't have any strength to recover. Every action a reflex, he was operating almost on impulse, his movements determined by the response of a reptile mind. And his reflex sent him stumbling directly to the pile of sheet metal scrap that was Crankshaft's office.

The same tin office he had hidden in as a child. He'd grown up there. At first, after the death of his father, he had played baseball on the lot next door all day and hidden at Crankshaft's at night. Crankshaft had known but never said anything. Later, it was the same tin office Mac had hidden in when the police were looking for him because he had escaped from the orphanage. Then he'd left town.

The door to the office was unlocked. Mac let himself in, stuck his head under the slop sink, and gulped down some water. His death march ended with three wobbly steps to Crankshaft's desk. Sitting on the edge of the chair, he slid open the top drawer, and pulled out a bottle of Crankshaft's bootleg corn liquor. He grabbed a cup off the desk, poured a shot, downed it and growled.

He made the effort to push himself back in the seat, but one of his hands slipped on the armrest and he held the other arm out to balance himself. His head pitched forward and hit the edge of Crankshaft's desk. He scooted the rest of his body up toward his head. His head stayed there.

●●●

Mac woke up wearing a pair of coveralls and lying in a cot hidden in the corner of the underground garage on Crankshaft's lot. From the trail of light cast down the ramp entrance he could tell it was afternoon. He lay in the shade staring at the ceiling until Crankshaft came down the ramp a few hours later and switched on the lights. Crankshaft got Mac some bacon and eggs from a diner, and Mac shared the story of his kidnapping and death sentence. If he had remembered anything about the walk home, other than his house having been firebombed, he would have bragged about that, too.

"What day is it?" Mac said.

"Thursday."

"And when did I get here? "

"Yesterday afternoon."

Mac hadn't been aware he had been asleep for twenty-four hours. He sat up in bed and began counting on his fingers.

"Three days, Crank. I was locked up for three days."

"Yeah, well you're lucky to be alive."

Mac looked at his bandage wrapped fingertips. "Crank, The Butcher knows who I am. He burned down my apartment. Chances are he knows all about me."

"What are you going to do?"

"If I don't kill him, he'll kill me."

"You don't have to kill him."

"Crank, if he knows all about me, he knows all about you and all my friends. I just disappear again; he'll start killing my friends."

"Then you have to kill him, but he's got about two hundred men. Those are pretty long odds if you can't get to him alone."

"You can't. I sure as hell can't. This guy's an enforcer, but he's also a ghost. Nobody knows who he is. Nobody's talking or they'd be in my shoes. Every time The Butcher makes an appearance, somebody dies, and nobody's aware of it until he's gone."

"And you don't know how to find him."

"Oh, I know where he is. I just don't know how to get in there." Mac sighed and rubbed his jaw.

"Give yourself a couple a days for a brainstorm, Einstein. They beat some of yours out."

"Can I borrow some change for the phone?"

Crankshaft nodded and waved to a pile of change on the worktable built into the wall. He shook his head back and forth to himself as he climbed the ramp back into the sunlight.

Mac climbed off the cot slowly, feeling his body. His throat hurt, he felt weak, his torso felt like he'd been through a wringer, his fingers hurt, his arms hurt, his hair hurt. Mac decided to stop thinking about things that hurt.

His feet hit the floor and they hurt. Grumbling, he stood up and got dressed. Mac kept an extra suit in the garage, and one in the trunk of whatever he was driving. He bought batches of suits in the same style at wholesale. The Bagman was hell on suits. Mac put on the only tie there, a faded yellow and brown, almost as ugly as his old one.

His part-time office was a pay phone in back of the Rexall Drug store on Lincoln. It took Mac a little longer to get there than usual. He climbed in his favorite booth in back, shut the door, and the fan in the tiny vent above him began to spin. Mac lit a cigarette so he could watch it work.

He tossed the match in the metal ashtray on the wall, put a handful of nickels into the phone and called the only other two people who might be in danger. Torch singer Coco Blue, Crankshaft's girlfriend, and Hunts Helms, Mac's old con man buddy turned newspaper public relations man.

Mac left a message with Coco's answering service. The good news was she was out of town playing Kansas City. He left a message at the city desk for Hunts then realized it was still too early for a night owl like Helms. He called him at home and missed him there, too.

The only other person he could think of that might be in danger was Mara Webb. He didn't think she was, but just the fact that he had gone out with her had put her life at risk, and she was living with the Butcher's gang. He wrangled her phone number out of his pocket, put in another nickel and dialed.

"Hello, is Mara there?"

"Nah, she's not here," the voice on the other end said, the same way somebody else might say *get lost*. Mac could tell it was Dutch Webb, the ex-wrestler.

"Well, when is she supposed to be back?"

"She's no longer with us."

"'No longer with us'? Is she all right?"

" She ain't coming back."

"Can I talk to Grinder?"

"Who wants to know?"

"Mr. Quirt." Mac gave the name of the fur thief he'd given Grinder.

"Quirt? You the guy with the furs?"

"I need to talk to Grinder."

"Um, well, unfortunately, Mr. Quirt…Uh, Grinder is no longer with the company. He's, uh, moved on to bigger and brighter things." With that last phrase, Mac could tell Dutch was forcing himself to sound upbeat.

"Thanks, but I'm only talking to Grinder." Mac hung the earpiece back on its prongs.

It was obvious Dutch was lying. When a successful mobster graduates to bigger and brighter things he, and all his friends, usually make sure everybody knows about it. But when a gangster "moves on," it's usually past this mortal coil. Chances are The Butcher had Grinder murdered for that little foul up at the Edgewater Beach Hotel. Or else Grinder had screwed something else up.

Mara wasn't coming back. She'd either been kidnapped or killed. He somehow knew that if she had left town, she would have left word for him. If Grinder was dead, then in all likelihood she was, too. Just for being Mac's friend.

He exhaled and kicked the door open with his foot. He wasn't thirsty, but he stepped over to the drug store soda fountain and got a milkshake. He had to get his strength back. He bought a copy of Argosy Magazine and wandered back to Crankshaft's where he picked up an empty suitcase.

"You don't have anything left to pack, do you?" Crankshaft said.

"Don't worry about me, Crank. I always have some cash stashed away, but it's a whole lot easier checking into a dive hotel with an empty suitcase than with no luggage at all. I just wish I hadn't blown my cover. Now, I'm back to hitting these guys from the outside."

He sounded more upset about the job than about the money.

●●●

After checking into the Davis—a hotel one cockroach short of being a hovel—Mac spent most of the day resting and in the phone booth, spreading word that he needed some career criminals for a job. When they got back to him, he talked to the right people and told the others the job was filled. He was calling in all his favors.

Word on the street was that Grinder, Mara, and Curtis "The Cleaver" Hatfield had been liquidated. Mac wanted to tear the phone off the wall, but his fingers started bleeding again.

The next day when he got out of bed, he was still sore but feeling almost human. He unwrapped the bandages from his head and fingers, and substituted for them with a fedora and a pack of Band-Aids on his fingertips. He had planned on just going through the motions that day, healing up for the next match with the Butcher, picking up a new gun, and a plan. But when Mac stepped out from under the faded awning of the hotel a shadow still hung over him.

Glimpsing up, he saw the hulks of Kerr and Tobar towering over him. Before Mac could say a word, one of them slapped him in the chest with a Colt .45 Snub-Nose wrapped in a shoulder holster. The other one put an arm over his shoulder and steered him toward a car parked across the street.

"What is it guys?" Mac said. "Look, I don't have a plan yet!"

Silently, Kerr or Tobar—Mac still couldn't tell them apart—opened the door for him and motioned for him to sit down. They drove in silence to Crankshaft's lot. The ace mechanic's tiny tin shack swelled beyond its four man occupancy. Coco was still on tour, but Mirella, Hunts Helms, Kerr, Tobar, Crankshaft and Mac all collected in the office and the edges of the tin stalls Crankshaft defined as a garage.

"It is time," Mirella said, sitting royally in Crankshaft's desk chair.

"Time? Mirella, I've got nothing! I've called in some favors, but we're talking about a big organization, at least two hundred men. I can dig up maybe thirty-five. Nobody knows anything about this Butcher guy, and he's almost killed me twice, before I even knew he was there.

"The stars say it is time," Mirella said. "The fortunes of those you have infiltrated have changed, even the one closest to you."

She was talking about Mara. There was a moment of silence before Mac spoke.

"But we need an army."

"Or one good soldier."

"Lady, Seargent York couldn't take out this crew. And he can aim a whole lot better than me!"

"I hate to ask," Crankshaft interrupted. "But what about all those old guys you pulled out of retirement from the O'Banion mob? That would at least be a start."

"Crank, those are some of the toughest old birds I ever met, but you're talking smash-and-grab when what we need is a complex heist. The Butcher has a plan, and a gang with at least two hundred members loosely situated all over the city, and he can probably call in more. The only people who really know what's going on are the ones who know what's locked up inside the Purity Meat Plant. Putting your headquarters in a slaughterhouse like that makes all the statement The Butcher ever needed to. If blood and guts are your front, there's no telling what they're hiding in back."

"I can get some of the Wacker Avenue gang over here, but it's the same problem," the ace mechanic said. "That packing plant sits like a fort in the wilderness."

Mac sat on the edge of the slop sink, lit a cigarette and glanced at the drawer Crankshaft kept the whiskey in. Something happened behind his eyes. He stared blankly at the space in front of him while the others continued to talk. Then, a few minutes later, he suddenly snapped his fingers.

"Waitaminute." Mac's eyes came back into focus. "What if we could kill two birds with one stone?"

Everybody but Mirella exchanged confused glances.

"I'm talking about bringing in the Chicago Outfit, Nitti's guys."

"Dangerous talk," Hunts Helms said. "I thought you didn't want to take sides on this one. Seriously, Nitti's mob is twice as dangerous as the Butcher."

"I'm not talking about joining them," Mac said. "I'm talking about using them."

"And how are you going to do that?" Crankshaft said.

"Mac McCullough can't do a thing, but Nitti's got a contract out on the Bagman. What if I were to offer the Outfit all the money the Bagman's stolen from them?"

"But, you don't have it," Crankshaft said.

"They don't know that."

"But what if they think it's a set up and don't bother to show?" Crankshaft's eyes half-rolled.

Mac reached around Crankshaft and opened the whiskey drawer.

"We'll give them an even better reason to show." Mac looked at Kerr and Tobar, then at Mirella. "You mind if I borrow the Katzenjammer Kids awhile?"

•••

A half hour later a hot rod Lincoln parked on the corner of LaSalle and Wacker Drive. Mac stuck a piece of gum in his mouth and offered some to the brothers sitting in the car with him, who declined. Then he looked at his watch.

"Banking business day ends at three o'clock. Our boy should be coming along any minute."

Nine minutes later a stout man in a suit and straw hat came out of 221 N. LaSalle, the headquarters for Frank Nitti's Chicago Outfit. Mac smiled behind the wheel as the man turned in their direction.

"Just grab him without anybody knowing it, guys," Mac said.

Kerr looked at Tobar. Tobar shrugged.

Kerr stepped out of the car as the man in the straw boater passed. He walked the same pace for about five steps, then caught up with the man until he was behind him. Standing just to his left Kerr tapped the man's right shoulder. As the man turned to his right, Kerr's arm swept around his shoulders and over his mouth. To the people on the street it looked like somebody greeting an old friend and putting an arm around him.

The man's feet kicked beneath him as Kerr walked back to the car with his hand clasped over his victim's mouth. Kerr maintained a grip so firm that the man's hat stayed on despite all his flailing. The Lincoln's back door opened, and the giant Gypsy threw him on the floor of the back seat.

Tobar planted a foot on the man's belly and smiled at him, before he stuffed a ball in his mouth and taped it closed. Kerr tied a neckerchief around the man's eyes as Mac started the car, and the struggling sounds of their victim were drowned out by the engine. Kerr and Tobar shoved the man back onto floorboard. Tobar crossed his legs and rested them on the man's stomach. Mac took Wacker Drive to Clark and headed back for Crankshaft's garage.

Kerr and Tobar didn't know it, but they'd just kidnapped Frank Nitti's accountant.

•••

Jake Guzic was a big man, both literally and figuratively. Not only was he the treasurer for the Chicago Outfit, but he was also their bagman for payoffs to the police and politicians. If you wanted to follow the money, he was the man to talk to.

And if the Outfit wanted to know where their money was, well, he was the only guy that really knew. Kidnapping Guzic was an instant death sentence, because without him the mob had no legal financial representation. Guzic knew too much. But Mac didn't want the information, he wanted its power.

With masks on, they locked the mobs "greaser" to a chair in the corner of the underground garage. The Bagman gave him some water, told him to shut up, and taped his mouth closed again, then hung some large tin signs from the ceiling to form walls so they wouldn't have to look at him. By the muffled groans from under the gag it was obvious Guzic would tell them anything they wanted to know. But Mac only wanted to know one thing, and the longer he waited the more willing Guzic would be to talk.

Still, The Bagman had left some tools and medical devices lying out on a table like they were going to torture the mob accountant, just for laughs.

Guzic awakened to a single bulb hanging from a wire, barely revealing a prison cell composed of junked, sheet metal signs. He struggled against his bonds but didn't have the strength to escape them. Glancing over at the tray in front of him, the powerful man shivered at the knives, pliers, razors, and a bloody hemostat Mac never cleaned for just such an occasion.

A man with a fedora and burlap for a face strolled into the room, ignoring the mob's treasurer as he straightened the tools on the rolling tray.

Jake Guzic's eyes bugged. He screamed a high pitched wail from beneath the tape across his mouth, jumping in his seat and pleading. Tears leaked from his eyes as he begged the mysterious interrogator for mercy. But the eyes behind the mask burned back at him, then almost smiled. It was a light of knowledge. The light of knowing what lives in the dark. The light of things no man should see, yet once seen, no man can forget.

Guzic wet his pants.

The Bagman tore the tape off his mouth. Guzic screamed, then tried to talk and the result was babbling. The man with the burlap face grabbed a handful of the accountant's hair, forced his head back and stared into his eyes.

"What's Nitti's home phone number? A number where I can reach him without getting the brush off."

"EN-EN-ENglewood three—seven, nine, three."

The Bagman slapped the tape back over Guzic's mouth and rolled the chair he was tied to across the improvised cell.

"I'll be back to deal with you later. You move—I feed you to the dogs."

"Jake Guzic's eyes bugged."

He pushed the tray of torture tools beside the cot, where it rattled and fell over. "Let me know which one of those you like. I got some friends that want to know."

The Bagman turned and stepped casually out of the room.

Guzic's eyes went wide again. He tried to scream. He pulled his legs up in front of him in the chair, curled up into a ball and shook. Then he stayed that way, still shaking.

●●●

The crowd at the soda fountain was thinning out as Mac made his way to the back of the drug store and his favorite phone booth. Pulling the ear piece from the prongs, he dropped a nickel in and dialed.

"Hello, Frank? Frank Nitti?" Mac said, like he was trying to recognize an old buddy's voice. "Hi Frank, you don't know me, but—" A bee's buzz cursed him from the earpiece. "Look, Frank! Frank! I got your accountant." The buzzing subsided. "Jake Guzic, I've got him."

Nitti's voice buzzed.

"Frank, Frank, Frank, let me be frank about this. The only reason I borrowed Guzic is because I think it's time for you and I to sit down and bury the hatchet, forgive and forget, let bygones go by so to speak— Forgive and forget, Mr. Nitti— It's the Bagman, Frank, and all I want to do is give you back the money I stole from Tommy Ahearn—Yeah, that was me— That's right, the bank job Tommy the Machine pulled… Well, I'm not only going to give you the ten-percent he would've given you, but I'm going to give you the entire take. You and I have just got to get along, but I figured the only way to get you to show up was to grab your accountant. And I think when I say that, you think, you know I'm right. We have a lot more in common than you'd believe, Mr. Nitti."

Mac made a face like he was sick to his stomach through the phone booth glass, but his voice stayed smooth and businesslike. The bee buzzed at him some more.

"Meet me. Back o' the Yards at the Purity Meats Plant on 43rd Street, tomorrow night at nine."

Bzzzzz. Bzzzzzzzz. Bzzzzzzz.

"Well, you can kill me if you want to, but we need to talk first. Remember, I'm putting up forty-thousand dollars just to have a chat with you." And with that sentence, Mac locked in the arrival of Frank Nitti and his armed guards.

The mob boss wasn't stupid. The Bagman had taken out the entire Slots Lurie gang all by himself, and Lurie's gang had been under the management of Nitti's Chicago Outfit. There was an entire section of the north side not paying protection money because this faceless Bagman came out of nowhere and threatened everybody. He had no respect. He was a danger to himself and others, no matter what side you were on. No, Nitti wasn't stupid enough to think the Bagman would be stupid. Crazy maybe, but not stupid.

Nitti failed to realize he could never understand Bagman's motives because the two men were driven by different engines. The Police Department had the same problem. They were trying to understand something Mac was just beginning to understand himself. The power of the King of Thieves was the balance between good and evil.

Mac pulled another handful of nickels out of his pocket and began pouring them into the phone. He needed a man on the inside—somebody that could park a car on the Purity Meats employee lot—and the only one he had left was Dutch Webb. He figured the ex-wrestler might not be too happy with his boss killing the rest of his roommates. There was a danger that Dutch might rat him out, but Mac's plan only involved Webb in the early stage. So if Dutch went in only pretending to be helping, he'd still do what Mac needed him to. It was a calculated risk. Mac dialed the number to Mara's old address.

"Hello, Dutch Webb—? You don't know me, but I need to talk to you and you alone. Anybody listening in on this line—? I need you to go to a pay phone on the corner of Paulina and Thirty-Fifth. From there I'll send you somewhere else. To make sure you're not followed. Make sure you're not followed. It involves Grinder Madlin."

"He ain't here."

"I know. The question is—what are you going to do about it?"

●●●

A half hour later he was back at Crankshaft's garage with the rest of the crew.

"Oh, no, not again," Crankshaft said. "You called up and scheduled another shootout? Last time you tried a 'plan' like that there was massacre in Bughouse Square!"

"We learn from our mistakes, Crank."

"You don't. You just made the same one."

"No, I didn't. Bughouse Square was full of innocent bystanders. This joint, nobody's innocent."

"So what's the plan?"

"I figure Nitti's guys will get there early. They'll all be stationed at the packing plant by seven o'clock because I told them to meet us at nine. That means all the workers will be out of the factory and just the gang remaining. I'll drive an old junker on the lot around 8:30. You'll be driving the Blue Streak for our getaway, and The Bagman will appear in the middle of the parking lot at exactly nine."

"You think you'll be able to just walk inside?" Crankshaft asked.

"Not without force."

"And Nitti's that force?"

"Something like that."

"So what keeps you from getting killed in the middle?" the ace mechanic asked.

"Ancient history," Mac said. "But I'll have to borrow another car off the lot."

"Ancient history, but you want to borrow a car?"

"Yup." Mac smiled. "Ever hear of a fire-ship?"

●●●

That afternoon Mac went to Mac's Tobaccos, the cigar store that acted as his legal front. The same day he'd met Mirella at the World's Fair, Mac had made the acquaintance of a gang of juvenile delinquent, newspaper boys and bribed them to create a diversion there. The little wise guys had to come to Mac's cigar store to collect their pay and had been hanging around ever since. Mac gathered them in the alley beside the store and asked who wanted to make five dollars. All eight hands went up. The kids formed a line to take the first dollar up front.

"Meet me here at six-thirty tonight, guys" Mac said. "There'll be a car waiting to pick you up and drop you off. And stay out of trouble."

And with that, Mac had hired the most inconspicuous lookouts in the business.

●●●

The first thing you noticed about the Back o' the Yards was the smell. Both sides of the street were lined with meatpacking plants, and almost every plant in the district had some sort of stockyard in back. The air hung thick with the scents of the beef, manure, steel, and blood that made up this part of the city.

The front of the Purity Meats Packing House was really the plant's loading docks with the gate to the small employee parking lot facing 43rd Street to its right. The packing plant faced north and covered almost an entire city block, with a decorative office on the left side of the building facing Paulina Street to the west. The employee entrance was on the right side of the building, by the employee parking lot. Beyond it to the east, a culti-

vated field faced Marshfield Avenue. Part of the field jutted onto the packing plant's property, creating a grass-covered patch between the city and
the slat-fenced stockyard behind the factory, where cattle grazed in a dusty
pasture that ran the length of the plant. And behind the roving bovines—
as if to taunt them—sat the final indignity, a glue factory.

Barbed wire topped the fences surrounding the employee parking lot,
making it look more like an army base—or a small prison—than a parking lot. The only ways into the building were through the office on the
left, or through the employee entrance on the right next to the parking lot.
The loading docks in front of the building were closed and locked for the
evening.

Any other place and Mac could have walked in, applied for a job and
snuck inside, but that was impossible with the Butcher in the back room.
Still, that didn't keep Hunts Helms and his buddy Phil O'Brien from walking in the door of the office ten minutes to closing time.

In contrast to Hunts' somewhat dapper appearance, Phil O'Brien looked
like an animal in construction clothes. Nicknamed "the Werewolf" by his
buddies because of the fur all over him, O'Brien had been a professional
street fighter before he'd settled down in Chicago to become a brick layer
and neighborhood terror. While the Werewolf wasn't exactly the poster
boy for mental health, he was sneakier and would draw less attention than
the giants Kerr and Tobar.

Hunts and the Werewolf were about to apply for a job. They knew they'd
immediately be told there were no openings—a fourth of the country was
out of work—but once inside, they could still ask to fill out some sort of
job application, or ask to use the rest room, or suggest they had important
news for a man named Smith. Given their varied backgrounds, the two
men could not only sneak in back individually, but they could stall for time,
or take prisoners.

●●●

Later, as the sun set on the city, the neighborhood shipments had
already been trucked and traffic was light, most of the meatpackers having
already headed home. A produce salesman led a mule cart down Paulina,
hoping to make that last sale of the day to families who sat on their front
porches trying to ignore the smell of the stockyards.

At seven P.M., a gang of children playing with an array of baseball equipment and barrel hoops hopped out of the back of a pick-up on the corner
of 43rd and Marshfield. The tiny troop, ranging in age from six to thirteen,
broke into separate groups. Three little wise guys with balls and bats made
their way toward the freshly mown field next to the parking lot.

The smallest of them, a six year old with blonde bangs and a red sweater four times his size, clambered up a tree in the center of the field. He sat on the highest branch that would hold him and turned, spying on the streets around him in every direction. Three of the younger boys pushed barrel hoops down the sidewalk with sticks, as the rest of the juvenile crew began wandering around the block.

Every time the kids saw somebody sitting in a parked car, one of the barrel hoops seemed to stray and fall right next to it. Two or three boys would gather around the hoop and fight about the actual distance it had rolled. The vehicle occupants never knew they were being watched. Within an hour, the boys had identified four different cars stuffed with mobsters.

Nitti's men hadn't been hard to spot. Their cars were too nice for the neighborhood. Two Lincolns and two Deusenbergs. One on each corner of the building.

The oldest of the boys reported the locations back to Crankshaft, parked around the corner on Paulina. Crankshaft waved his arm from behind the wheel of the Blue Streak at several cars parked behind him. Those cars were stuffed with suspicious characters, all of them men who hated Frank Nitti or the Butcher. Old Irish members of the O'Banion mob worked side by side with Black and Jewish gangs from Philwell Street and half the career criminals in the city. All of them putting aside their long-held feuds because they hated the man at the top of their heap.

●●●

Precisely at eight o'clock, Dutch Webb appeared at the packing plant's gate driving a maroon Model-A Town Car with the windows open. Dutch spoke to the guard at the gate through the window and then drove inside, circling the sparsely filled lot as if looking for a parking space.

At that exact moment, a child's scream cut through the air, and the boys in the field ignited a roll of firecrackers. The cattle penned behind the building bawled as the herd swelled and shifted, stirring up dust that drifted in a low wave toward the glue factory. As the guard turned to see what the racket was, a figure slid from beneath the circling car, hit the concrete and rolled into the shadows beneath a brand new Hudson Essex by the employee entrance. Webb parked the Model-A in the center of the lot and headed into the building.

If Dutch hadn't ratted Mac out, the ex-wrestler would be exiting the building from the other side on Paulina in a half hour and taking the trolley home. If Dutch stayed inside, it meant the Butcher knew trouble was coming.

A train rattled by and faded in the distance. The sound of birds chirping and children playing cut an eerie beat between the moments of taut silence. Nitti's men sat hunched in the corners of their cars, reading newspapers, smoking cigarettes, and flicking ashes out the window. The blonde boy in the oversized red sweater sat on his tree branch, his head turning like a bird's as he glanced up from a five-and-dime pocket watch in his hand.

Dutch Webb stepped out of the office entrance of Purity Meats and onto Paulina Street. As he crossed 43rd, he tipped his hat to Crankshaft and gave him a nod. Crankshaft nodded back, still not sure Dutch was on the square.

There was still a little daylight as the clock struck nine. The little wiseguy in the tree raised one hand in the air stiffly, then threw it down like the flagman at an auto race.

A wobbly figure wearing a mask that looked like a burlap bag popped up in the back seat of Dutch Webb's Model-A. One of the figure's arms waved back and forth as he wobbled, like he was trying to get his circulation going.

"Hey, lookit!"

"The Bagman!"

"Aw it's just some guy in a scarecrow suit!"

"Don't be a dope! That's the Bagman! I seen him before!"

The Bagman's name echoed down the street. Every smart aleck kid in the neighborhood pointed, yelling and joking with each other from across the lots and hollering his name. Nitti's men in the front of the building pushed their newspapers to the floorboards. Starters whined, and callous men reached for the guns under their lapels as the engines revved. Wheels spinning, a black Lincoln tore down the street and through the front gates of Purity Meats.

The guard at the gate held out his hand and screamed for the car to stop, but was forced to leap to the side as the vehicle missed him by inches. The guard pulled his service revolver and fired at the rear of the Lincoln as it tore its way across the lot.

Machinegun fire scorched the air, and a hail of bullets struck him in the back as the second car pulled up behind him. The guard collapsed across the intersection, and the Deusenberg bounced three wheels over his body without altering its course.

The first car circled to the right side of the sparsely filled lot, the second circled to the left. When they had almost reached the point where Dutch Webb's Model-A was parked between them, both cars stopped and opened fire.

One of the larger dead-end kids grabbed the blonde child out of the tree and swung him to the ground. Everybody in the neighborhood hit the dirt as an orchestra of leaden death tore through the Back o' the Yards.

Thompson Submachine guns, automatics, and revolvers riddled the

Model-A with a barrage that droned for a full three minutes. Glass shattered, tires hissed and metal ripped as bullet holes stitched their way from end to end of the sedan. Hot lead popped black and gray holes through the car's body until the Ford's maroon paint job ceased to exist. The steady pulse of gunfire slowed, sped up, and then stopped, with the occasional shot still going off like the last of a batch of popcorn. Two or three gangsters kept shooting at what few parts of the car hadn't been hit yet.

The masked man in the car kept waving his arm and bobbing.

"What the…"

"There ain't no way."

Cursing, the squads on both sides jumped from their cars, staying low, and warily approaching the Model-A. A squinty-eyed gangster emptied an automatic at the masked man's head. His fedora blown off, the figure seemed to lean back a little before bobbing forward with his left arm still swinging like a metronome.

"Something ain't right, Professor."

The Professor squinted more, lowered his head and took a step forward. As he stepped closer, he began to see the last ebb of daylight glow through the holes in the figure's clothes. The mask had been torn to rags. The left arm had no hand, and the Professor noticed a series of diagonal lines bulging through the torso that resembled a man whose entire skeleton was made of ribs.

A goon with a pencil-thin mustache stuck out his chest, sidled up to the car and hit the masked man across the face with an automatic.

"Ow!"

The professor came up behind him and grabbed the figure in the car by the shoulder. Its coat fell off revealing a series of thin, rusty metal bars. Somebody else tore the remains of the shirt off to reveal an industrial metal spring, coiled forty-two inches in diameter, which until last night had been sitting in Crankshaft's junkyard. The figure's arm was a foot-long coil somebody had tied to the larger one with bailing wire.

"That ain't the Bagman. It's a spring," the goon said.

While the gang gathered, milling and shifting around the car to inspect the spring-loaded Bagman, the professor opened his mouth to speak. But before he could say anything, the sound of a heavy engine revved from across 43rd street and ruptured the moment. The goon squad spun to see a small shipping truck parked in the drive of the meat plant across the street. Tobar stepped out of the truck smiling, with the engine still running. The big Gypsy pulled a match out of his pocket. Members of Nitti's gang began to lose interest, bickering, asking questions and yelling orders.

"Guys I think we been—" Again, the Professor didn't have time to speak. The air popped. They felt the *whoosh* of fuel igniting and a sudden warmth swept over them from behind. The truck parked on 43rd had burst into a ball of flame.

Across the street, Tobar bent and reached in the only hole left in the fireball, the car's open door. The engine revved high and stayed there. The sound drifted over Nitti's men like a Wagnerian opera as Tobar backed away from the intense heat. Then he leaned into the fire and slapped the gearshift.

The fireball launched itself, bouncing across the street and into the lot.

"Ambush!" the Professor screamed.

The burning truck careened off one of the fence poles just missing the gate. But, the force of the collision bounced the truck back on course, straight down the middle of the parking lot. Nitti's men ran in all directions, firing across the street, but the big Gypsy with a mustache wasn't there.

The truck slammed into the remains of Dutch Webb's car and exploded, careening across the lot into one of the mobster's sedans. Metal wrenched and fire flashed beneath The Deusenberg before it burst into flame. A wall of smoke and fire separated Nitti's men from the street.

"C'mon! Inside!" The Professor hustled the remaining crew toward the meatpacking plant's employee entrance. Blasting the lock with his gun, he screamed, "It's a set-up! Kill 'em, kill 'em all!"

●●●

What the Professor didn't know was that while his men had been shooting at an industrial steel spring, The Bagman had slid from beneath the Hudson Essex where he'd hidden and picked the lock to the employee entrance.

He had bought just enough time to get a glance at the place, and was literally playing both ends against the middle. If things went according to plan, Nitti's men would come in behind him, and the Butcher would think the Bagman was with Nitti. But Mac had to stay just far enough ahead of Nitti's gang for them to believe the Bagman was working with the Butcher.

Somewhere in the middle, Mac was supposed to meet Hunts Helms and Phil O'Brien.

●●●

Kneeling in front of the employee entrance, The Bagman felt the tumblers of the door's lock click as Nitti's gang began to gather around the spring decoy in Mac's clothes. He eased the door open, slid inside and closed it behind him.

The warehouse was dark, but the last glimpse of evening scattered light from the vented windows two stories above him. The Criminal Detective stood to the right of the door with his revolver in his hand before his old cat burglar instinct kicked in, and, without even thinking about it, he found himself making his way across the warehouse with his back to the rear wall. Judging from the reflections, the back room was easily a hundred feet wide. The entire packing plant was enormous.

As shadows ran over his burlap face, the moonlight glinted off his .45, and steely gray eyes burned in the spaces between the light. Something rattled to his left, the same sort of sound a mouse might make or a building settling. Without moving, he waited and determined a series of chains hanging from the ceiling, used to move cow carcasses, had caught the breeze.

Mac heard yelling outside. An engine revved and something exploded. Mac's fire-ship. Nitti's men would be breaking down the door any minute. With the employee entrance behind him, the rear of the building stood to the left, the Paulina office nearly half a block away in front from him.

"If it was me," Mac thought, "I'd hide in the corner, as far away from the employees and the front office as I could." But, he was supposed to meet Hunts and Phil O'Brien somewhere inside, so he bounded up the hall toward the front office instead.

A single bulb hanging forty feet in the air was all that lighted the next room. Mac leapt in sideways and dove for the cover of one of the meat cutting tables. Nobody was there. *Weird.* Slowly his eyes adjusted to the light and his head cleared the top of the table.

Mac wished it was still dark.

Standing up, he realized he was in what the meatpackers call the Butcher's Room. Large wooden tables and chopping blocks sat in rows. Racks hung from the ceiling to hang the meat on. Conveyer belts on wheels as big as Mac stood along the walls of the room. Across one of the conveyer belts lay a butcher knife that looked like cricket bat had mated with a machete. Four feet of blade and two feet of handle, for chopping carcasses as they rolled down the belt.

Mac heard something to his left and turned to see a man across the hall with his arm extended from the opposite door and a gun in his hand. The Bagman stared up the barrel of the Colt Automatic aimed between his eyes. The man with the automatic's finger tightened on the trigger.

Something went *thump*. The automatic clattered on the ground, and the man with the gun's head hit the concrete with a disturbing *thud*.

Hunts Helms stepped out of the doorway behind the body, holding his automatic like a club. Phil O'Brien stepped out behind him.

"Fancy meeting you here, tall, dark, and ugly," Hunts said.

"Front office empty?" the voice beneath the mask asked.

"All clear. I sent the cleaning lady home early." Hunts pointed toward the South wall. "Thataway?"

"You sure the office is clear?"

"Nobody visible on the entire west side of the building."

"Damnit, that means they could be behind us." Mac pounded on an imaginary desk with the bottom of his fist, glanced at the southeast corner behind them, directly opposite the front office, and then at the exit on every other wall. He could hear Nitti's men breaking in the employee entrance behind them. Mac waved his gun in the direction of the exit on the south wall, the back door. Or so he thought. "Giddy up."

Even as the three men hurtled down the hallway, Nitti's men burst into the butcher's room behind them. The Professor and his gang stood in the dark just like Mac had a minute ago, listening. One of them found the light switch, clicked it on and off repeatedly. The lights were out. One of Nitti's men turned on a flashlight and searched the corners. The braver ones headed west, across the building for the front office. Luckily for Mac and his crew, the plant had more echoes than a haunted house.

Nitti's men continued searching the gigantic room, clearing the one desk, searching its drawers and ransacking the shelves on the walls.

"Search the building, not the drawers!" The Professor screamed.

● ● ●

Mac and his crew exploded into the back room of the building. Then they smelled it.

Mac froze like a statue. Hunts and O'Brien stopped so fast they were backpedalling. The air was moist with the smell of blood and disinfectants mixed with steam exhaust. The ground was wet. Hunts and O'Brien jerked their heads away, Hunts with his gun hand over his nose.

A bulb lit the room from the rear, shining directly in The Bagman's eyes and pitching a dim red light on the stained hooks and fixtures hanging from the ceiling. The blood stains in the corners and crevices lined the slanted floor in dark umber tones and crusted around the drain in the center of the room. A few seconds later, the silhouettes of twenty armed men appeared on the other side of the room. A tall, dark figure in gray stood on a gutting table like it was a pedestal with arms akimbo. The figure made eye contact with The Bagman.

"Out of the frying pan and into the slaughterhouse," Hunts said.

"I always liked the sound of 'abattoir' more," the masked man deadpanned.

The tall, dark figure said nothing for a moment, then a grating voice cut across the room.

"You enjoy playing the fool, don't you, Bagman?" The dark figure pointed a finger through the murky light at Mac. "Well, this is your last joke."

"Yeah, like you could stop me," the masked man said. "This seal walks into a club—"

"Shuuut uuuup!" The Butcher screamed. His high-pitched, nasal voice echoed through the warehouse. "Shut up, you insufferable moron!"

"Whoop, now you're getting personal," Hunts said.

One of the Butcher's men stepped forward from the side and slapped Hunts across the face. Every muscle in the con man-reporters body stiffened as he glowered back into the mobster's eyes with rage.

"No joke, Butcher," the Bagman said. His voice was hard and imperative. "I'm going to kill you."

The Butcher's manic laughter filled the room. His goons laughed along like a dictator's audience forced to applaud.

"Seriously? A man that runs a cigar store is going to take down a mob. Even when you're serious, you're a joke—"

The Butcher continued to speak, but Mac wasn't listening to him. He was listening for Nitti's men, trying to figure out when they'd bust into the room. His head turned to the side in an effort to hear them better.

"…are you listening to me!" The Butcher screamed, louder than ever before.

"Oh, sorry. No, not really." Mac could hear Nitti's men, trying the door handle behind him. "I mean, that's a nice costume and all, but you're still just another crook."

"Fool!" the Butcher growled. "You're not going to hear anything again."

"What?" Mac held a hand to his ear. He was stalling for time.

"I'm taking the city before Prohibition ends! There's a fortune to be made, and you and I both know it. Bootleggers will become captains of industry, respectable citizens."

"And you think I'm funny. Look around, buddy! This is Chicago! Blood is an industry. The Outfit won't even let the Mafia in!" The Bagman almost yelled over his shoulder.

He had been stalling for time, but he couldn't have done it any better. The second Mac had stopped talking Nitti's men broke through the door behind him.

"McCullough, The Bagman, Frank Nitti—you 're all dead!" the Butcher announced.

And that was the first thing Nitti's men heard.

The Bagman grabbed Hunts and O'Brien by their belts and, jumping, shoved them into the right hand corner. The slaughterhouse exploded with gunfire.

Snatching the one rolling rack left on the floor, The Bagman tossed it in front of Hunts and O'Brien for the little cover it offered them. Gunfire flashes lit the scene like a strobe, every movement revealed like a slow silent movie. A gun would flash and any standing figure might be crumpling to the floor the next time Mac could see. Slow motion violence moving way too fast.

There was no cover in the room except for the lousy tin rolling rack and one table nailed to the floor in the middle of the room. O'Brien the Werewolf grabbed one of Nitti's men and turned, using him as a shield as bullets popped in the man's back. Mac jumped into one of the concrete gutters that funneled blood to the center of the room, lying on his back and firing at anyone that wasn't Hunts or the Wolfman. A body fell on top of him. The Bagman used it to shield himself, reloading and firing from beneath the pale face of the corpse.

The Criminal Detective eyed Hunts and O'Brien in the corner. They'd gotten the same idea, and two more bodies lay across the top of the rolling rack. World War Two broke out as men fired at men standing directly in front of them, all lined up like two rows of ducks at the world's deadliest shooting gallery. Gunfire flared unabated for minutes before it began to subside. The shooting slowed down to a *pop* every second or two. Five men still stood in the room. Two on the Butcher's side, two on Nitti's. Mac and his buddies knew better than to stand up in the middle. The others hid themselves behind the bodies of gang members, firing because they didn't know what else to do. The Bagman stuck his head up.

Just in time to see the back of the Butcher disappear behind his pedestal. Mac pushed the body off him and fired twice. The Butcher's last two men went down screaming as The Bagman gave chase, almost stumbling over the blockade of the dead between him and the back of the room as he reloaded on the run.

What was left of Nitti's mob let him go. Even if Nitti did have a contract out on the Bagman, in this gang's eyes the King of Thieves was on their side now.

●●●

A wooden cattle chute ran out the back door. A door stood open next to it. The Bagman jumped off the platform in back of the slaughterhouse and through the door. The outside air cleared his head a little, but it still smelled like blood and chemicals. Then he smelled the manure. The cattle in the stockyard bawled and mooed, shifting in the sparse grass of the stockyard.

The Bagman wedged his hat on and rushed for the gate. Mac loved cows.

The only time he'd had to deal with them was when he'd been squatting as a hobo. They made good cover.

He opened the gate to the stockyard like an old hand, grabbed a rope off one of the fence posts and began to follow the herd flowing in front of him. The Butcher had left not so much a trail, but more of a mess, cattle running and bouncing off each other. Mac trotted across the yard, slapping cows out of his way and hollering, as he slid to the opposite edge of the fence. Nobody shot at him.

Even kneeling by the rear gate of the stockyard fence, he could see the Butcher's footprints, and the open door to the glue factory in the moonlight. The Butcher was doing the opposite of what The Bagman would have done. He was holing up instead of taking off. Rookie move.

The Criminal Detective heard a horn honk and glanced to his right to see Crankshaft idling down Paulina. The ace mechanic was circling the block. The Bagman stood up, waved at the driver and pointed toward the glue factory.

All the lights were out inside. He could easily be seen outside. Inspired by the cattle, Mac stopped at the door and stuck his hat through it first, like a cowboy in a Western waiting to see if somebody would shoot at it. Waiting an uncomfortable second, he shoved his hat back on his head and ducked in the door.

●●●

The glue factory was smaller than the Packing Plant by far. Giant air vents on the second story, no windows, just slats of light. Mac always eyed the exits first but couldn't locate any, just darkness and dust motes dancing in the slats. But they were dancing fast, too fast for the dead late-summer air. Mac backed toward the wall like the burglar he was, and into something metal. A box on the wall with electric knife switches on it, the big kind with handles on them.

The Man of Steal threw every switch. Machinery began to drone, and the dim lights above came on in three stuttering sections. Normally The Bagman was a creature of the night, but this time so was his prey. So he changed the game.

With every machine in the glue factory grinding and clanking, he didn't have to worry about being quiet. The Bagman sought the high ground. Above him stood a screen metal floor twenty feet wide that ran around around the top of the room, most likely for the supervisors to observe the factory workers below. Bounding to a metal staircase in the shadows to his left, he took the steps three at a time to the second floor, and hit the metal screen platform sprinting. Swinging himself around the iron corner post hanging from the ceiling that held up the walkway, he vaulted toward the south, back end of the room. Metal barrels lined the walls. Between the barrels sat vats of chemicals, whose chutes and tubes ran down to bigger vats and the industrial machines spitting below.

The Man of Steal kneeled between the barrels and waited. He'd played this game before. The drone of some of the machinery sank to an impatient buzz, wheels still turned and metal still clanked. Even with the noise, The Bagman could still hear the ticking of the time clock below him. The police would soon be on their way.

The clock kept ticking.

For a moment he thought about tying the rope low across the stairs he'd ascended. Then he remembered the game he was playing, thought better of it and stayed still. Sirens began to drone two notes in the distance. He sat listening, accustoming his ears to the sounds and rhythms of the factory, waiting to hear one that didn't fit. Between the beats of the mixing machine, a piece of tin barely clattered off some heavier metal. Slowly, the Butcher stepped out onto the walkway with his head hanging.

"You can come out now, Mac. There's no time," a familiar voice said. A siren wailed in the distance. The Butcher pulled the hood off with one hand, and a head of auburn hair fell out from beneath it.

"I kind of figured it was you," The Bagman said, and stepped out onto the platform. "You'd be the first one they'd let live—if they didn't know who you really were."

"You were right, Mac." It was Mara. "It *is* a big joke." She was crying.

"No. No, it's not," The Bagman said. "Look, Mara, I don't know what happened to you, but we can get you some help. It's what I do, I'm good at—"

"No." She laughed sardonically. "It's a joke." Mara Madlin slapped Mac's open hand and turned away, taking a few steps before leaning on the platform's arm rail.

Mac held his hands in the air, showing he meant no harm. She stopped and turned back, her mournful eyes looking into the icy blue ones in the burlap mask. She opened her mouth as if to say something, then took a deep breath, and, diving, launched herself over the handrail.

The rope Mac grabbed by the stockyard gate had already been tied into a lasso. The King of Thieves swung the rope over his head and down at the plunging Butcher, but it wasn't waxed like the rodeo rope he practiced with. The loop at the end twisted into a figure eight., missed her ankle and slapped the side of her leg.

Mara didn't even scream. She landed headfirst in the industrial bone grinder.

Mac turned his head and tried to not to hear the popping and cracking as the unconscious body twisted to pieces in the machine's grinding gears.

"Look Mara...we can get you help."

The pieces shredded into ever smaller fragments, and soon the grinder sounded dry again.

The Bagman stood there, not seeming to notice the rope hanging out of his hand. He stared into space blankly a second before glancing down at the grinder. Shaking his head, he trudged toward the Butcher's gray hood lying on the walkway and picked it up. He shook his head again and made his way downstairs. Moving with an uneasy rhythm, Mac yanked the knife handle switches on the wall down. The lights went out and the machines shut off. With the Butcher's mask still in hand, The Bagman lumbered through the glue factory's front door.

The Blue Streak pulled up directly in front. The Bagman opened the car door and sat down, closing it as Crankshaft floored the gas and shifted into the next gear. Mac pulled his mask off and stuck it in his jacket pocket.

"The Butcher's dead," he said, staring at the cowl he'd kept in his hand. "Fell into a bone grinder."

"Damn! Dust to dustier." Crankshaft spun the wheel and aimed the Blue Streak for home. "Who was it?"

"Nobody," Mac said, almost to himself. "Nobody I knew."

The End

THE CAPTIVES OF RAVENSWOOD

Most people who had just had everything they owned blown up by their girlfriend, who later turned out to be a psychotic maniac, would probably be down in the dumps for a few days. Mac McCullough was not most people.

With the things Mac had seen and learned growing up on the road he had come to know death and insanity almost like personal acquaintances. He didn't particularly like them, he didn't particularly fear them, but he knew they were there. Fortunately, these things had driven Mac to the "shooting dice" school of thought regarding his own mortality. "When your number's up, your number's up." So he didn't worry about it too much, until he was in trouble.

He'd found himself moping around the house all Friday night, but upon picking up this morning's paper he found just the thing to cheer him up. *Gordon of Ghost City* starring Buck Jones was playing at the Saturday Matinee; a Western with rustlers who hid out in a mysterious ghost town. Mac loved cowboys, especially the Saturday Matinee. For him it was like being a kid all over again, except he'd never really grown up. He was barely self-aware enough to sit in the balcony where he wouldn't be seen.

So when the picture ended and the theater cleared, nobody expected a one-hundred-and-ninety pound, six-foot bandito with a barrel chest to step out on the street with a throng of children shooting six-guns at each other with their fingers.

Mac fired a few shots back and forth with the rest of the kids, blew the smoke off his fingertip and then holstered it. The kids laughed and waited for him to draw again, all of them but one. A boy of about eleven on the corner.

He was screaming.

"Lemme go! Lemme go!" And Mac heard the familiar sound of flesh striking flesh.

Two men with their hats pulled low surrounded a raven haired youth on the corner, one pushing, one pulling, forcing him into the back of a black Model-A sedan. Mac almost pulled his real gun, before he thought about the innocent bystanders on the street. It didn't matter. He was already sprinting across the intersection.

Sliding in the air like Ty Cobb, Mac stomped the calf of the man nearest him and hit the ground rolling on his shoulder. The second man stomped at Mac's head, but it was too late. Spinning, Mac bowled up against the thug and rapped him in the groin with his fist. The child broke free and sprinted across the street bawling. The thug clutched his crotch and fell to his knees as the car's wheels squealed in the background, leaving him behind.

Mac pounded the first man with a fist like a mallet, then stood up on the corner trying to get a license plate number, but the Model-A's driver knew his stuff and was already twisting around the next corner. Noticing the man to his left still clenching his groin, Mac threw a roundhouse that lifted him up in the air and out on the sidewalk.

The kids gawked in shock a moment and then began to scream and cheer from in front of the movie theater. Glancing out of the corner of his eye, Mac saw Harrigan, the local beat cop, hurrying down the street, and almost broke into a chase for the kid who had already run away. In Mac's line of work, the less the police thought about you, the better off you were. He'd been hoping to have time to question the suspects, but his long held rule of trusting no one in blue had kept him out of jail so far, and at this point was a trained response.

All of this because Frank "Mac" McCullough had been crazy enough to put a bag over his head seven weeks ago and take on the neighborhood protection racket. A career criminal, McCullough had been working his way up the racketeering ladder as a bagman, when they'd offered him a promotion. But then they sent him to break his uncle's legs. Instead, Mac McCullough had broken his associate's nose and stolen his car. So it was fitting that the local press had dubbed this new mystery man the Bagman. He'd been through a series of masks since, but now wore one that looked like a tight burlap bag wrapped around his head.

The mask had been given to him by a Gypsy fortuneteller. A real one, who told real fortunes and knew things nobody in else in the world could. At the World's Fair, Mirella the Traveller had told him he was heir to the Gypsy legend of The King of Thieves. Mac didn't quite believe he was the King of Thieves, but he did enjoy balancing the scales of justice when somebody else had their thumb on them. And besides, the mask she had given him was *silk-lined.*

The Man of Steal had never investigated a kidnapping before, and a list of problems he had never confronted ran through his brain like ticker tape. He could always call his newspaper buddy Hunts Helms and get the line on the men who had been arrested. But as far as the men already out there, *kidnappers always told their victims not to call the police or the newspapers.* People who wanted to keep their kids alive didn't talk. And Mac had never met a kidnapper in his life that was sleazy enough to admit to being a baby trader, which left him with nothing.

•••

Crankshaft's car lot was closed for the day, and Mac didn't much feel like hanging around a junkyard by himself waiting to get advice, so he went to Mac's Tobaccos, the cigar store he owned that acted as his respectable front. A single story slot on Lincoln Avenue he rented by the month, it wasn't much, but it was great place to get information. Newspapers were sold there.

Not that the Chicago dailies could ever give Mac the information he wanted, but the newsboys could. Mac had offered a gang of delinquent newspaper boys a chance to make a buck at the World's Fair a couple of weeks back, and now he couldn't get rid of them. As a favor to his clerk, Mac had agreed they shouldn't come in the store unless he was with them. There had been a little shoplifting problem. The boys were wild and, in most situations, maybe more trouble than they were worth, but they had their eyes on the streets. Some people in the city let children see things, because they thought kids didn't count. Mac loved proving those people wrong.

As he watched them gathered around the alley near Lincoln and Paulina, they reminded Mac of himself at their age, back when flipping baseball cards was just as important as shooting dice. The kids were doing both, and hawking the latest edition right next to Mac's store, where he was supposed to be selling newspapers, too. Mac had thought about it and come to the conclusion that since he wasn't exactly running a legitimate business he had no right to complain.

"Who's winning?" Mac said.

"Nobody," a six-year-old boy in an oversized red sweater said. "We was playing poker, but Rube was winning too much, and we figured out the cards were marked, so now we're just trying to divvy the stuff up."

"What happened to Rube?"

"He ran off. Joey beat him up. Give him two weeks, and he'll be back."

"I hope so," Mac said. "Speaking of disappearing, I was wondering if you boys had heard anything on the street about kidnappings, or if maybe some of your friends, or some other kids might be missing?"

"Ruben," the child in the red sweater said.

"Shut up, Pee Wee," said a serious looking older boy, Jimmy. "You mean school kids, right?"

Mac did see a part of his childhood, not the best one. This kid was already drawing the lines that would separate him from the rest of humanity.

"Yeah, school kids."

"Couple o' kids that go to St. Joseph's. One of 'em Golden Gloves, ain't been there in weeks."

"Any of these kids got names?"

"Knuckles."

"That's not a name, Jim, that's a prison introduction. I mean like a given name, a last name."

"Oh, his name's Terry Wiles. I known him since I was a kid."

"Long time, huh." Mac smiled with half his mouth. "You said 'a couple of kids.' You happen to know the name of the other one?"

The older boy's mouth slanted. He tilted his head and held his hand out. Mac almost smiled and tsk-tsked with his head. Jimmy knew Mac was pumping them for information, he wanted his cut. Mac slapped a dollar bill in the older boy's palm, and then held his hands up in a surrender motion so the other kids wouldn't rush him. Jimmy stretched the bill in his hands and looked over both his shoulders, daring someone to step in front of him.

"Terry Wiles and Beanie—I don't know his real first name—Beanie Lundquist, they both live on Marshfield." Jimmy rattled off addresses and descriptions of the houses.

Mac handed him another buck, told the kids to stay out of trouble, and then headed down the street.

•••

Jacob and Mabel Wiles' home sat on the second floor of a respectable three flat less than a block away from Mac's Tobacco shop. That night, Mac McCullough let himself in the front entrance and made his way up the stairs to the second floor. He pulled a mask that looked like a burlap bag out of his pocket and pulled it over his face. He wedged his fedora on over it as he normally did but flipped the bill up, thinking The Bagman would look friendlier that way.

The Criminal Detective rapped five times on the door and put a saintly conman's face on under the mask, hoping it would transfer to his eyes. He heard the sound of voices inside, then steps coming toward the door. A haggard man in khakis and a t-shirt opened the door. His eyes were rheumy, and his five o'clock shadow stuck out in patches where he'd missed shaving.

"Hi." Mac waved his hand as he spoke in an almost childlike manner. "Would you happen to be Mister Jacob Wiles?"

"You son of a bitch!" Wiles threw a hard right.

The Bagman caught Wiles fist in his left hand, forced it in front of him and then held it there. Placing his other hand gently on Wiles chest, the masked man pushed him into the room.

"I'm here to help, Mister Wiles."

"If you hurt Terry, I'll kill you," Wiles rumbled.

"I didn't take him, but you've given me one less question. He has been kidnapped hasn't he?"

"Yeah, about a week ago." Wiles sighed and deflated in Mac's grip.

"Jake is everything all ri—" A blonde woman wiping a coffee cup with a dishtowel stepped into the room. She dropped the cup. It hit the floor with a cracking sound, but rolled back on its handle.

"It's all right, Misses Wiles," the masked man said.

"Y-you're that Bagman, aren't you?" She said.

"Yeah."

"I've seen you in the papers," she said, shaking. "Just—what are you? They say you're crazy."

"They could be right. Listen, I know your kids have been kidnapped and I know you can't go to the police."

"Why not?" Mister Wiles said. "We reported it as soon as possible."

"Wait a minute, you called the cops? Didn't you get a ransom note telling you not to tell them?"

"No, we didn't get a ransom note at all."

The Bagman stood there stunned a moment, and then realized they were staring at him. He really had expected a ransom note. And if they had called the cops, why hadn't anybody been looking for the missing children? He excused himself, and made his way down Ashland Avenue taking off his mask in an alley, so he could use the phone in a drugstore. After giving the operator the Lundquist name and address, he simply spoke to Beanie's parents on the phone. They hadn't gotten a note either.

These children hadn't been kidnapped at all. They had disappeared.

Mac stepped outside, lit a cigarette, and huffed smoke angrily through his teeth. McCullough had a soft spot for kids. As the saying goes, he'd been one himself, and it was not a time he always looked back on with fondness. He tossed his butt and chewed his lip a minute, then went back inside to call an old friend.

Hunts Helms was one of Mac's pals from his previous, but not so scrupulous, life. They had met selling oil wells that didn't exist, to financiers who couldn't believe they didn't. When Mac had returned to Chicago, he'd been surprised to find Hunts working as a public relations man for the city. In a way it was the same old con. Hunts was a real life reporter, who just happened to sell the city of Chicago in all his reports. It wasn't really journalism, but Mac figured Hunts wasn't that much of a journalist, anyway. The one thing the reporter in the gray suit did have, however, was the scoop on every bit of business in every city office. Mac went back inside and called the "journalist."

Hunts answered the phone energetically, but replied to Mac's questions with a whisper and one hand around the mouthpiece. Sixteen children had been reported missing by their parents in the last two weeks. The police had told him they were on the case, but they didn't really have anything to go on, just missing kids.

Part of the problem was the economic depression. A lot of parents went so far as to kick kids out of the house because they couldn't afford to feed them, as was the case with some of Mac's newsboy buddies. A lot of "respectable" types might even report the children missing the next day or two, but he doubted it happened too often. Even if half the kids missing ran away from home, it didn't add up. Mac juggled the numbers in his head, and still came up with the same conclusion. The kids had disappeared.

That night the big man hit all of his favorite sleazy, crime-ridden speak-easies, trying to find anybody that knew anything about anything. Apparently, Mac's favorite watering holes weren't sleazy enough. Dejected, he strolled home in the early morning hours. As he slept, children screamed in his dreams.

And he was one of them.

●●●

He woke up too early to do anything. So he ate breakfast without tasting it, and read the newspaper without thinking about it, then waited till noon and started hunting for stool pigeons. A whole day was spent on trolleys, trains, and in cabs. He sweet talked and muscled every grifter, junkie, alcoholic, and low level pervert on the street—not to mention the working girls—and still came up with nothing. He was headed over to Crankshaft's to find out what the ace mechanic thought, when he saw the gang of little wiseguys in the alley again.

"Hey, Mister McCullough," the youth in the red sweater said, his blonde hair hanging over his eyes.

"You can call me Mac, Pee Wee. I was thinking about that conversation we had yesterday, and I was wondering if—"

"Millie Baumgarten's missing," Pee Wee interrupted.

"Somebody else you know?"

"Yeah, Millie Baumgarten," he said as if Mac should already know.

The rest of the gang idled up behind the kid with the blonde bangs that hid his entire face. They practically already had their hands out.

"Millie Baumgarten—" Mac said. "She lives in the neighborhood, too?"

"All the missing kids live around here," a boy wearing glasses with the frames taped together said.

"'All' of them? You guys know more?"

"Terry Wise, Beanie, Stretch Stine, Suzie Calvin—" The boy with the glasses had pulled a list out of his pocket that had at least fifteen names on it. "...and Mildred Baumgarten."

"Yeah, and Millie," Jimmy, the serious older boy said.

Mac nodded and stared at the boys, but something was wrong with the tone of their voices. Having been both kid and a conman among conmen, Mac had a fairly accurate built in lie detector, and something didn't feel right. The little delinquents had never lied to him before, but then again, they'd never had to. Like most street kids, the wiseguys were fiercely independent and had no problem telling anybody to go perform acts a whole lot worse than "jumping in the lake." Maybe the kids had just presented it wrong, but something was odd about it.

"This Millie, anybody know where she live?"

The boy in the glasses beat everybody to the front of the line. Mac slapped a buck in his palm. Specs gave Mac an address on Byron Street, almost right next to the two previous victims. The big man told the kids to watch out for each other as well as themselves then headed for Crankshaft's.

The ace mechanic was closed and already gone for the day. Mac considered hanging around because Crankshaft sometimes came into work at night, but decided against it. It was too early to go home. He didn't feel like hanging out in any more speakeasies, alleys, or dens of depravity. Maybe he could learn something if he tried a different approach with one of the other victim's parents.

●●●

The Baumgarten residence was a modest one story bungalow. It needed a paint job but seemed respectable enough. Mac went without the mask this time, thinking the parents might be more willing to talk to another victim than a masked man. He rapped on the door, and a beleaguered looking man in shirtsleeves and suspenders opened it. He had a newspaper and a pair of horn-rim glasses in his hand. Mac introduced himself, sort of.

"I heard from some of the neighborhood kids that your daughter is missing. My name's Bernie Lundquist. My son disappeared last week, and I'm trying to contact the parents of the other missing children so we can find out what happened."

Baumgarten stiffened for a second when Mac mentioned his daughter, as if maybe somehow surprised. Mac eyed him a moment, but couldn't get a read on the man's response. As much trauma as he'd seen, Mac still had trouble reading people's emotions in troubled times. Everybody reacts differently. Some people need time to spell things out.

"Please, call me Nathan, Mr. Lundquist."

"Bernie."

Nathan invited Bernie inside with a wave of his arm, and then waved again at the chairs in the living room, inviting Mac to sit down. He offered Mac a glass of water and Mac declined. Then they sat down.

"I'm afraid I didn't notice Millie missing until yesterday afternoon," Baumgarten said. "The last time anybody saw her was in school. I just finished reporting her missing. The police said I had to wait twenty-four hours."

"So when did you call the police?"

Mister Baumgarten started to answer and then stopped. He tried to fold his paper, but couldn't get it right and wound up shoving the whole thing beside his seat before answering.

"As soon as she went missing," he said.

"When was that?"

Baumgarten's eyes went up under the lids like he had to think about it, before he finally held up a finger and said something.

"Yesterday afternoon, about three-thirty."

"And the police told you to call back. When you reported back today, what did they say?"

"Not much. I asked and they said they had a detective on it."

"Do you remember the detective's name?"

"No—no, I was quite distraught by the time I could get anybody to talk to me, but the man on the phone said they had a lead in the missing children case."

"Really?" Mac said. "They called it 'the missing children's case'?"

"No, no, they didn't call it that. They called it the…" Baumgarten snapped his fingers a few times. "They called it 'missing person cases in the city,' like Millie wasn't even a child. Are you telling me there are more children missing than Mildred?"

"Yes, there are," Mac said. "Quite a few. That's why I didn't expect the city to just name it "the missing children's case." I've got a friend with Chicago public relations, and they're usually a little more creative when it comes to making bad things sound good."

"Oh, my."

Mac followed up with questions about whether Baumgarten had seen any strangers or anything odd in the neighborhood, but the man assured him he hadn't.

"I write articles for trade journals, so when I get home from work to relax, I'm usually just writing more. Other than trips to and from work, or the Post Office, I don't see the neighborhood that much. I'm sorry I'm not more help. I'd do anything to get Millie back home safe. I'm so worried. I haven't been sleeping; I can't concentrate at all—" He was still rattling off a list of personal woes even as he rubbed his face and began to yawn. "I'm sorry. My whole world's just been torn apart."

"I understand," Mac said.

"Please, let me know if anything develops, or if there's any way I can help, anyway at all. Please, anything."

They shook hands. Mac thanked Baumgarten and left. He swung by Crankshaft's Car Lot but the ace mechanic wasn't there. Mac knew he wouldn't be able to sleep, so he went back out to question people in the same speakeasies and alleys he'd explored all day.

The problem was Mac didn't even know how to bring up the subject. Normally, if he wanted information about a crime, Mac just went to a bar and asked the shadier clientele if they had any work for him. But in this case, what was he going to do? Ask if somebody had any really horrible jobs that would give him nightmares for the rest of his life? He knew half the lowlifes in the city, but he still didn't know anybody that low.

And if he did, he would have already taken them out.

He needed a motive. He'd asked some of the most defeated working girls he knew, and offered good money, but ironically, even they had been appalled at the thought of the child slave trade. All of them, but one.

"Hello, and what's your name, little girl?" Mac said in a voice that turned his own stomach. Of course, being long overdue on both "little" and "girl," the woman in the alley had already given his indigestion a head start.

"Misty," the peroxide bomb said.

"Misty, huh? I like that." Mac had never heard such a name before, much less ever heard of anything verging on two-hundred pounds referred to as 'Misty'. "That short for Misterella?" he said, thinking of fairy tales. If he'd had a glass slipper, he'd have defended himself with it.

"Oh, you're a funny one." She covered her teeth when she talked.

"Probably a little funnier than you want, Misty, I'm looking for something a little... No, a *lot* younger."

"Mister, you're sick." Misty's face twisted into a knot. "The Outfit would kill anybody plying the trade with little kids."

"That's what I thought, Misty, except somebody's been kidnapping the little bastards all over town—and I want one."

"You can't get one around here, Mister."

Mac breathed a sigh of relief, and began to reach for his wallet to give her a tip, until she opened her mouth again.

"Honestly, I wish I could help you, Mister. 'Course, with all the kids out here, they'd prob'ly be better off with a good pimp anyway."

That's when Mac realized she hadn't twisted her face up in disgust at the idea of kidnapping, but because she was upset she wouldn't be making any cash. He turned, pushing his wallet further into hip pocket with his thumb, and walked away. She screamed names at him for half a block. No one was around to notice and, to Mac at least, none of the names sounded as bad as Misty's.

Mac wandered around the neighborhood the rest of the night, not really paying attention to where he went, and going over the possible motives for a ransom-less kidnapping.

The black marketers were making too much money off booze, tobacco, and everything else that fell off the back of the truck to risk hanging for kidnapping. As bad as the Chicago Outfit was, they still had too much Old World family pride to be moving kids out of the neighborhood by the busload. Mac even popped in on a couple of drug dens near Chinatown but when opium is your main source of income, you don't exactly have the energy to work on much else.

He had been shooting two days and rolled nothing but snake eyes.

He wanted to go home and sleep, but he wanted to go home to his apartment, and it wasn't there anymore. His psychotic ex-girlfriend had blown the place sky high.

He definitely did *not* want to go back to his room at the Davis Hotel, the dive in which he was currently forced to reside. Mac knew he wouldn't be able to sleep, anyway.

So he walked to the corner of Lincoln and Addison where the El station's lights fought with the shadows of the tracks. Rounding a hot dog stand and making his way down a long dark alley, the big man paused beneath the sign for Crankshaft's Car Lot, picked the lock on the gate and let himself in. Locking the gate behind him, he then headed for the secret underground garage where they hid the car Mac had stolen from the Chicago Outfit only a few short weeks ago. The theft that had begun the Bagman's career, and had also bagged him some very nice wheels; the Graham Blue Streak Eight.

Already a speedster, Crankshaft had modified the Blue Streak into a performance vehicle that held tighter in the corners, and was faster in the straights, than was legal on the streets. And if that wasn't enough, he'd installed a separate tank on the engine, so its fuel could be spiked with nitrous oxide or alcohol when even faster speeds were needed. With bulletproof shielding surrounding the engine, and mirrored glass so no one could see the inside, Crankshaft had been forced to tone the car's original paint job down. Secrecy still required the Blue Streak only be driven at night, but Crankshaft had some of the fastest cars in the city on his lot for the daylight.

In the underground garage, Mac leaned back in a deck chair he'd brought down for just such an occasion and began reading a copy of Dime

Mystery. His disappointment grew as he realized the story was more of a fake alien invasion than a mystery. The mystery seemed to be that some editor thought it made sense.

●●●

McCullough awoke to a black hand shaking his shoulder. He sat up erect, swatting Crankshaft's hand away as he jumped upright in his cot, gasping.

"Oh, Jeez, Crank! I thought you were an octopus!"

"Yeah, well I'll let you get your coffee yourself," Crankshaft said.

"Sorry, Crank, it's those damned Shudder Pulps."

Hunts Helms, Mac's old conman buddy turned reporter, laughed from beneath his straw hat and picked up the magazine, pointing at a picture of a boneless man crawling across the floor.

"'The City of Crawling Death!'" Hunts quoted from the title. "C'mon, Mac, this guy couldn't catch anybody."

"Yeah," Mac sighed. "I don't think I was dreaming entirely about myself."

"Now, don't get yourself too worked up, but I think the city solved the 'Crawling Death' crisis a few years back. It's the all the other deaths piling up around here causing all the problems."

"Morning, Hunts." Mac said, shaking his head. He was already clothed under the blankets. He straightened his tie before he stepped out of bed. "What's the good word from the city?"

"Not much. They're keeping the kidnappings under their hat, but the parents are getting antsy. They're tired of being told to wait and getting ready to hit the newspapers. The papers have been told to keep a lid on it as long as they can. Maybe forty-eight hours, tops. The cops don't have anything, but they're driving unmarked cars around the city patrolling for the kidnappers."

"So nothing's changed."

"The patrol cars are new. I thought that might make you feel better, but after checking your reading material I'm not so sure." Hunts shook a pack of cigarettes and took one out of the pack with his mouth. "Maybe you should stick to detective stories, Mac."

"No, I don't think so."

"Obviously, or you wouldn't be reading that crap," Crankshaft said.

"No, I'm not talking about the crap I read, Crank. I'm talking about labor."

"What, you pregnant?" the ace mechanic said.

"Only with brilliance, old man, only with brilliance. Whoever's stealing those kids is using them for child labor. At least that's my guess. Whoever it is, it's either part of a very select, very sick and probably rich crowd or they're taking them out of town. Given the state of the nation, I'm willing to bet it's child labor."

"And you got all that out of an octopus dream?" Hunts puffed out smoke as he talked.

"Yeah, I guess I did. The arms represented the labor."

"Man, that's weird." Hunts was one of the select few that knew Mac had been 'crowned' the King of Thieves. He also knew Mac went into trance states and came out knowing things he couldn't possibly know.

"Of course, you could have just picked up a newspaper in the last thirty years. There's big money in slave labor, and who's easier to enslave than a kid?"

Silence hung thick in the air as Mac stared at a space before him with regretful eyes. He almost shook his head again coming back out of it.

"You know what your problem is?" Crankshaft started to tell him, when he was interrupted by a high-pitched, helium voice screaming on the car lot above them.

"Mister Crankshaf'! Mister Crankshaf'!"

Mac and Crankshaft's eyes went wide. Hunts gave them a curious look. Crankshaft tossed Mac a hat, and all three bounded up the garage ramp and to the junkyard.

"Mister Crankshaf'! Mister Crankshaf'!" Pee Wee screamed, beating on the side of the tin shack Crankshaft called an office. The boy was excited and his ragamuffin demeanor looked worse than usual. His hair stuck up in back. Blood was smeared on his forehead and the knife in his hand.

Mac was first to reach the scene.

"Pee Wee! What happened?"

"Some grown-ups tried to grab me. I stabbed one of 'em and got away, but they're fighting Specs now! They're gonna kill Specs!"

"Where are they, Pee Wee?" Mac grabbed the boy by the shoulder.

"Corner of Addison and Ravenswood!" Right by the tracks that stood above Crankshaft's car lot.

"Get The Blue Streak, Crank!" Mac yelled.

"It's daytime!" the mechanic said.

"Get the Streak!"

Crankshaft shrugged his shoulders and broke into a sprint back underground.

"Hunts, lock up and don't drink all Crank's whiskey." Mac tore his way to the front gate, and ran down the alley toward the intersection. Hunts grabbed Pee Wee by the shoulders and began coaxing the knife out of his hand while he distracted the boy from the Blue Streak's exit.

In back of the junkyard, a gray shimmer bounced off a paint job designed not to be noticed. The two glass eyes of the car's headlights peered out as if from hell itself. Then one big eye, the Blue Streak's reflective windshield, shined the world back on itself, as if to remind it that the doors to hell lock from the inside. The driver's window rolled down revealing a man with eyes like a human fly, Crankshaft and his reflective goggles.

"Lock up!" The fly yelled. Hunts kept distracting the child.

"Where'd you get him, kid?"

"Through his hand," the boy said, with a stabbing gesture. "I couldn't reach his heart."

"I believe it, kid. I believe it." Hunts patted Pee Wee on the back. "Ya done good, kid."

●●●

Mac sprinted under the tracks and bound across traffic to the intersection where the newsboys hawked their papers. Just in time to see a boy being forced into another Model-A.

The boy, Specs, kicked against the car and both men, stabbing at their eyes with his fingers as they pushed and pulled at his bony appendages. The spare change rattled from the newsboy's pockets as he fought, but his glasses stayed on his head. Mac hurdled the hood of a car and leaped for the driver just as the kidnapper's door slammed in back. Specs glanced at the big man with eyes full of fear as the car spun its tires, and took off down Lincoln Avenue.

The Blue Streak roared from under the El tracks. Crankshaft yanked on the emergency brake and spun the wheel. The car slid in a circle and came up right next to Mac on the corner. The Criminal Detective leapt in and pointed.

"They went down Lincoln!"

The Blue Streak sped down the block, just in time to see the nondescript Model-A turn right on Belmont. Crankshaft took the turn and slowed two cars behind the escaping vehicle.

"You thinking what I'm thinking?" the ace mechanic said.

"Never. But we should probably just follow them and see where they go."

"Exactly."

Crankshaft let the Model-A lead them out of the city headed south. At first tailing them was easy, he simply stayed a car or two behind, and always just behind any hill or turn that might be available, but not too close. Thirty miles outside of the city they hit a farm road, and things got harder. The Blue Streak slowed, idling down the road in third gear almost a quarter of a mile behind the kidnappers, as Crankshaft limited himself to following the cloud of dust they stirred up for another thirty miles. As they reached the

"They went down Lincoln."

Indiana border, the car turned down a dirt road that was little more than two ruts worn in the ground. Crankshaft stopped the car as they turned onto the road, still staring at the clouds of dust in the air and waiting for the Model-A to get a little further away.

"I'm guessing farm labor, huh, Crank?" Mac said, slapping his hands together.

"But it's too late in the season for corn. It's too late in the season for anything, really." Crankshaft eyed the scrubby fields around them. "Except maybe pumpkins and it's too early for that."

"Maybe things were so bad they didn't have anybody to bring the summer crop in."

"Or they're planning on planting something else, later." Crankshaft held up a finger and almost sang as he spoke, "Maybe when nobody is looking."

The two men made eye contact, and snapped their fingers at the same time.

"Drugs," they said in unison.

"And you can hide a lot of drugs in the middle of a cornfield," Mac said. "Take it slow, Crank."

The kidnappers' cloud of dust led them another ten miles before it finally stopped, thinned, and began to dissipate across the dry air of the autumn plains.

"Wait here, Crank. I'll check things out from behind the corn."

Mac slid out of the car and drifted between the walls of browning corn stalks, cutting across the corner of a field. Nearing its edge, he grumbled about his suit and began crawling on his belly. From his vantage point in the plow rows, Mac watched two men carry Specs from the car to an old farm house. There was nothing strange about the large toolshed and two outhouses in the small lot behind it. But next to the house, a truck sat hitched to an enclosed shipping trailer; not the kind of thing you'd use to ship produce, but just perfect for livestock.

And Mac didn't see any cows around.

A gigantic barn with flaking red paint sat a hundred yards backstage from the rest of the scene. Farm equipment and tractors weren't visible, but they could be in the barn. Though somehow, Mac doubted it.

He crawled back into the corn, stood up and began treading his way toward the center of the field. Forcing his way through a jungle of dried stalks, he could just make out an almost square-shaped mound in the middle of the field. Like somebody had planted a storm-cellar or a garden apartment, underground—right in the middle of the field—and then spread mud and grain all over it, so the structure above had no visible edges from above. The Midwestern version of an underground adobe house on the outside, Mac doubted it was a garden apartment inside.

He banged on the door. Nobody answered.

The door was bolted by two heavy Yale locks and a crossbar. Mac paced back and forth beside the structure, then stopped and placed his head against the side of the building looking for deformities. A few seconds later he walked ten yards and peeled some of the mud off the building. Then he yanked a vent cover off. He lit a match and stuck it inside. Nothing exploded and nobody shot at him. Sliding inside head first, he was greeted by something a little sweeter smelling than corn as he rolled to his feet.

Opium. He'd stumbled into a heroin ring.

Industrial growth lights filled the back half of the warehouse, where poppies grew clumped together in giant wooden boxes shelved on the walls and tables like tiny farms. The front of the warehouse was a laboratory. Beakers and tubes sat next to sinks on rimmed metal tables. The rest of the hideout trailed off to the east, a giant underground field with burning bulbs for suns.

On the lab table, some strips of paper that looked like gum wrappers were filed in a cardboard box. Mac opened a strip of the paper and poured the white powder onto the table. He thought about tasting it with his finger like he'd seen the police do, but he had no idea what heroin tasted like to begin with.

Checking his wristwatch, The Criminal Detective then climbed back outside and wedged the vent cover on, before seemingly floating back to the car where Crankshaft waited.

"Opium, farmer must really be hurting for cash," Mac said. "Pull into the corn field. I think we better wait for the rest of night to fall."

Crankshaft pulled the Blue Streak into the field.

●●●

An hour later the night was pitch black. Mac and Crankshaft crawled to the edge of the field, hiding in the same stalks of corn the kidnappers used to camouflage their deadly crop.

"I can see the light on in the farmhouse from here, but that's about it. You?"

"Three, maybe four men inside, but I'm just guessing from the shadows."

"You can see at night with those goggles on, Crank?"

"Better than most, yeah. I treated the lenses."

"Could be somebody upstairs asleep, too," Mac said.

"Want to find out?"

"I don't know." Mac turned over in the dirt and sat up, fishing in his pockets. He pulled out a coin and flipped it in the air, then caught it and slapped it on the back of his hand. "Check out that barn first. Free the kids."

"Oh, my lord. You *did not* just flip a coin to make a decision did you?"

"Yeah," Mac said. "But I forgot it's a two-headed coin. We still have to get the kids out first otherwise they're just targets and hostages."

"I hate it when you're crazy and still right. That kid with the glasses is still in the house, though, and there could be others."

"You take the barn. I'll take the house." Mac pulled his mask out of his pocket, pulled it over his head and wedged his hat on tight.

"We could both take the house," Crankshaft volunteered.

"No. They probably have a man watching the kids, and that means hostages, too. Check your watch. We'll both break in in exactly ten minutes. And keep things quiet."

"I don't know how to pick a lock."

"Knock out the guy with the keys, Crank, knock out the guy with the keys," Mac said as if he had memorized it from the burglar's rule book.

The King of Thieves was true to his legend as he broke into a crouching run and stopped at the corner of the house without making a sound. He turned back toward Crankshaft and put a finger to his lips, signaling to keep quiet. Crankshaft ran the borderline of the field for fifty yards then sprinted toward the barn.

The Bagman skulked his way to a shaded bay window. Peeking in through the corner of the curtains, he saw Crankshaft had called it right. Four men sat inside, two playing cards, two smoking and drinking. The talk was neither happy nor loud.

"I ain't too confident about this payoff, Earl."

"C'mon, Slats. We got four farms. We got free labor."

"But, we're too far up north. The weather ain't right fer this."

"You tried shipping opium into the United States from a foreign country lately? It's next to impossible. And, none of the rubes out here would ever be looking for such a thing."

"Somebody's gonna follow those kids."

"Who? A quarter of the country can't afford to feed the ones they got. And all's we grabbed was street trash. Nobody cares about a few missing kids. If they did, there wouldn't be so many of 'em."

Mac McCullough wanted to start shooting through the window, but the Bagman knew better. The Man of Steal made his way around to the back of the house. A series of concrete steps ran up to a screened back porch. Mac ignored the steps, sat on the porch, propped the door open and slid inside. In one motion he twisted, stood up and was already by the back door.

Leaning toward the window to his right, he peered in over a kitchen sink. A table stood in the middle of the room with a bottle of bootleg whiskey on it. A coffee pot stuttered on the stove. Somebody would be coming in the room soon to pick it up. He had to move fast. He glanced at his watch.

It was time.

The Criminal Detective pushed the screen door back in one quick motion so it wouldn't squeak. His leather-gloved hand gripped the interior door handle loosely and twisted. It was open.

He could hear banging on the walls upstairs. The Bagman eyed the whiskey on the table and a small frying pan hanging on the wall. He pulled the frying pan off the wall and stood behind the door. Voices blathered on the other side of the swinging door; one of them came down the hall toward the kitchen.

A tall man in a shiny suit came through the door and stepped immediately toward the whiskey. The masked man tapped him hard, twice, with the frying pan; two bruises, one less concussion. He caught the man, but his victim's unconscious feet scuffled on the fake tile. The Bagman dragged him to one of the chairs, sat him down and lowered his head to the table gently, then stood behind the door again, frying pan in hand.

The coffee began to boil over. He didn't make a move. Coffee broiled for five minutes before footsteps trickled back down the hallway.

A second man in shirtsleeves with oily black hair stepped through the swinging door, glanced at the coffee pot first, and then saw his friend unconscious on the table. Still gripping the door, he jumped back in surprise, shoving Bagman into the corner behind it.

The Bagman shoved the door the other way, hard.

The man with black hair stumbled sideways, knocking over the coffee-pot as he fell. His eyes and mouth wide, a vowel sound began to eke from his throat. The man with the burlap face grabbed him by the collar and punched him in between the eyes before the sound could become a scream.

Backpedalling to the door, The Bagman could hear voices in the front room, but nobody else seemed willing to check on what had happened in the kitchen.

Grabbing the whiskey bottle off the table and brandishing it like a club, he walked briskly up the hallway. At the end of the hall he knelt on one knee. He didn't want his reflection to be seen in the same living room window he had used to spy on the other two men in the room.

A chubby man in wide suspenders sat in an overstuffed chair with his back to the same wall Mac hid behind. A thin, young man in a black suit tapped an empty glass on the table impatiently as he spoke.

"I'm not going in there. Every time one of you mugs messes something up, I gotta take the blame. It ain't happening anymore. It just ain't."

"Aw, lighten up, Harry," the man in the chair said, drinking whiskey out of a tumbler. "Is it their fault they don't know how to make coffee?"

"Yes! It is!" The young man insisted with a mixture of shock and exasperation.

"Aw, quit yer whinin.'"

The masked man stepped around the corner and into the batter's box, swinging the bottle hard at the man sitting in the chair. It buried in his face with a thump and rolled across the floor, as the Bagman hurdled the card table toward the young man in the black suit. The masked man began to reach for his revolver in midair, but Harry didn't draw a gun. He grabbed the card table instead, and, slinging it between him and The Bagman, made a break for the staircase.

Halfway up the stairs, the Man of Steal grabbed him by the ankle and dragged him back down the steps. Harry rolled, his arms flailing, trying to grab the rungs beside him as the big man shoved him back down the stairs. As Harry bounced downstairs, he grabbed Bagman's ankle with one hand, and tried to drag him down with him. The Big man pushed the kid lower on the steps with his other foot, then kicked him in the jaw. Harry rolled over once, then slowly slid down the remaining stairs on his face.

The sound of a struggle and a muffled scream emanated from the door down the hall. Most likely the boy Specs, bound and gagged, screaming for help or a warning. Mac hesitated a moment. Normally, he'd just kick in the door and start shooting, but he was still trying to be quiet and if he kicked in the door there would be shooting. In order to keep the gang in the barn from taking the rest of the children hostage, he needed to do this without any gunfire warning them.

The King of Thieves massaged his jaw in thought for a moment, then approached the door. Standing to one side, he knocked on it like a salesman.

•••

Crankshaft knelt outside, by the corner of the barn and in the shadows of the hayloft above him, listening. Just opening the hayloft door would make them aware of his arrival. And there was only one way inside the barn besides the hayloft, two broad double doors that would announce a man's entrance like a theater curtain being raised.

He could hear the children inside whispering to each other, but he couldn't hear what they said. The kids had to be under guard, or they wouldn't have bothered to speak in such low voices. After a few more minutes, the ace mechanic was able to identify the occasional grumble of an adult male and the sound of cards being slapped on a table. The watchmen were playing Spades.

Crankshaft had the same problem as Mac. He had to operate without alerting any of the gangsters The Bagman was currently dealing with. He knew Mac would probably just walk in, start playing cards and then somehow end up beating everybody in the room over the head with the card table, but he also believed Mac was blessed with incredible luck. As a man who'd spent two years in the trenches during the Great War, he'd never considered himself lucky, just a survivor. And has far as he was concerned, living was not just surviving.

Mac thrived on chaos. Crankshaft thrived on the mechanical.

A small Army Surplus medic's kit hung over Crankshaft's shoulder by a wide strap. The ace mechanic unsnapped the bag's flap and rooted around inside. Ignoring the medical supplies strapped to the sides, he pulled out half-a-dozen metal balls, each about the size of an egg, and held them up in the moonlight to determine what color they were. The white eggs were flash grenades, the blue ones smoke bombs. The hay in the barn being a fire hazard, he put the flash grenades back in the bag. He wanted to rescue the kids, not barbecue them.

Reaching in his coverall pocket, he clenched his trusty "slapper" black-jack in his hand. His jaws flexed as he clenched his teeth, apparently coming to some sort of decision. Inhaling deeply, he stepped away from the doors and around to the side of the barn. His back to the wall, he stomped against it three times, and then waited.

Muffled voices fluttered through the cracks in the walls, a questioning tone and then an order. Crankshaft raised the blackjack over his head and became a part of the wall. A man with an automatic in his hand came around the corner, cursing in consonants under his breath. Glancing up, the man saw Crankshaft in his alien-looking coveralls and reflective goggles and stopped, hesitating for just an instant. The Blackjack came down hard.

Crankshaft dragged the unconscious kidnapper in front of the barn doors and laid him down in front. He took a deep breath and stepped back around the corner, where he kicked the wall three more times, and waited. Two different tones came from inside this time, almost in whispers. Crankshaft heard the footsteps, but remained positioned around the corner.

A stout, muscular man, in a suit too small for him, stepped from between the barn doors and stumbled over the body. Gasping, he managed not to fall down. But as he stared down at the body, the blackjack came down hard again.

Crankshaft left the unconscious man's body lying where it fell. He made his way back to the corner, and kicked the outside wall again, three more times.

He didn't hear any voices this time. Not a peep, which was exactly what he wanted. No talking meant he was down to their last man. The ace mechanic placed himself directly in front of the barn's entrance. The hinges squeaked as the man inside edged the door open and tried to peer outside into the darkness. Slowly, he stuck his head out.

Crankshaft slammed the door on it twice, holding it closed the second time. Releasing the door, the unconscious gangster slid to the ground with a *thump* as the ace mechanic rushed into the room. Scanning the inside of the barn to make sure it was clear, he glanced toward the north wall, and stopped, stone still.

Cages ran the entire height and length of the wall. At least sixty frightened young eyes stared back at him with questioning looks. Every one of them chained and gagged in their pens. Crankshaft put his finger to his lips, signaling to stay quiet. Several of the children nodded at him and he nodded in reply, before stepping back outside the door and pulling a set of keys from the last unconscious gangster's pocket.

One long chain ran the length of the cages, acting as the bolt that kept the pens latched, and then looped into the next row of cages below it. Crankshaft opened the padlock and dragged the rattling chains out in increments. As he made his way from one end of the room to the other, he used a separate master key to uncuff the children from their cages. A boy in a torn dress shirt yanked the tape from across his mouth.

"Gee, thanks Mister! I thought we were goners."

"Quiet!" Crankshaft gently slapped him on the side of the head, and some of the other children backed away looking frightened. The Harlem Hellfighter pointed to the corner of the barn. "Stay here and stay quiet. We still have to escape."

The cluster of children already freed edged toward where he pointed, removing each other's gags and rubbing the circulation back into their wrists, while Crankshaft made his way down the row of cages, unlocking the remaining prisoners. The boy that had spoken first made it his job to hush anybody else that tried to talk. Crankshaft smiled and gave him thumbs up, before returning his finger to his lips again.

But as the chains ceased to rattle, something pierced the silence through the barn door. Punches, kicks, and gargles. Crankshaft knew a fight when he heard one. Four shots fired outside and flecked paint burst through the barn walls from the bullets. Another shot fired, and Crankshaft finally drew his automatic.

Quiet or not, he wished he'd brought a Tommy Gun.

● ● ●

"Yo, boss! Ya better get down here!" The Bagman said in a voice that wasn't his, from outside the bedroom door. "There's a couple o' cars and a bunch of flashlights shining all over the center of the cornfield!"

The only answer was silence. Something in the room rattled, and the muffled voice screamed again. The Bagman stepped back down the hall and mimicked a voice as if it were far away.

"Those cars, they got sirens! Sorry, boys, but I'm out of here!" He slammed his hand against the wall as if he were slamming the door downstairs, then tiptoed back to the bedroom door, standing to one side.

The muffled screams had stopped, but something in the room clunked. Footsteps sounded toward the door, the handle rattled and it opened. A portly man in a wrinkled shirt with stains under the armpits appeared.

"What are you guys talkin' about. I don't see nothing—"

A leather clad glove punched the man in the heart. He stumbled backwards, gasping, and the other gloved hand pulled an uppercut up from the floor. The man with the armpit stains landed on the floor with a hollow *thump*, unconscious and spread-eagled on the floor.

Specs was still squirming on top of an old brass bed to the left of the door, his hands tied behind him to the frame. The Bagman untied the boy's gag. Specs opened his mouth and a red rubber ball appeared between his teeth. Bagman pulled the ball from his mouth and went to work on the ropes tied to the bed frame.

"You all right? They do anything to you, kid?" Bagman asked.

Specs, wary as to whether or not his situation had improved at all, only stared at the Bagman.

"Good, I need you to keep quiet," Bagman said, freeing the boy's hands. "We're probably going to have to rescue a bunch of other kids in the barn. You feel like being a hero?"

The boy shrugged his shoulders and rubbed his wrists.

"Yeah, me either. But sometimes, you just gotta." The Bagman slung the unconscious man over his shoulder, dropped him on the bed and began tying him to the brass bed frame. The boy remained silent until the strange masked man had finished. The King of Thieves grabbed Specs by the hand and led him down the stairs, stepping around the assortment of unconscious thugs. "I've got just one question for you, Specs. How did you manage to keep your glasses on through all this?"

The boy smiled at the use of his name, and a man asking questions instead of threatening him. Reaching under his long hair, Specs pulled a piece of masking tape from behind his ear identical to the tape that held his hornrim glasses together.

"Not bad, kid. Not bad at all. I hear they got elastic bands now some of those college athletes wear. Maybe you should look into that. Hey, can you pull the laces out of that guy's shoe? We need to tie these idiots up or they'll just be more trouble."

Eight minutes later the house was secure. Mac led Specs outside and told him to hide in the hedges by the side of the house until he heard a whistle. The big man swiveled his head, scanning the area, and trotted off toward the barn. Edging around the corner, he saw a stack of unconscious men lying in front of its twin doors.

"I hope you got the guy with the keys, old man," Mac muttered to himself, edging toward the door. Reaching for the handle, something grabbed him by the leg and twisted. The Bagman burst into a flailing pirouette, tumbling toward the ground as a knife tore at his face.

•••

The biggest of Crankshaft's victims was more than wide awake now, adrenaline rolling him around the yard like a panicked puppet as the Bagman's head and arms dodged between the stabs of the blade. Throwing an arm up at the last second, the knife slashed deep into Mac's forearm. He kneed the man in the groin like it was a reflex and rolled.

The two men bounced over each other in the yard, struggling and slashing in a ball of dust, dirt and hay. Mac kept rolling, still on the defensive, until he was wedged against the other unconscious mobsters with nowhere to go. The slasher's other hand splayed, fingers wide, digging under his bulging lapel.

The Bagman grappled the wrist of the kidnapper's knife hand with both of his, and rolled in that direction. The knife tumbled off into the dirt as the two men continued to roll themselves toward the barn, until, bouncing off it, they separated. The man with the burlap face recoiled off the ground and into a standing boxing pose, only to see his muscular opponent pull his revolver.

With no time for thought, The Bagman somehow leapt and got part of his left hand wedged between the gun's hammer and the firing pin. The fleshy part of his hand between the thumb and forefinger hurt even with the gloves on. It took all his will not to snatch it away as the hammer snapped twice on his hand.

Managing to wrap his hand around the man's gun, Bagman punched him in the gut. The angry assailant yanked on the trigger and the gun blasted four times, but Mac still holding his gun hand, forced the barrel away. The two men connected with simultaneous punches to the head and began wrestling on the ground. Rolling away and charging again, The Criminal Detective grabbed the man's gun hand and a harmless shot went off in the air. The kidnapper poked his spread fingers at the Bagman's eyes, forcing him to roll backward. He pulled the criminal along with him.

A muffled shot popped in the darkness, flashing between the two men's chests, and the slasher's limp form collapsed on top of the masked man.

Mac pushed the body off with his bloody arm and awkwardly climbed to his feet, struggling toward the barn, afraid the shots had alerted more kidnappers. Yanking the door open, he looked up the barrel of Crankshaft's gun the second Crankshaft looked up the barrel of his. Tense muscles unlocked.

"Almost got yourself shot, smart guy," Crankshaft said.

"Take a better old man than you," the Bagman scoffed.

The two men holstered their guns.

"It's OK, kids!" Bagman held up both hands as if making an important announcement. "We don't want to hurt anybody. We just want to get you guys home."

Most of the children already had them surrounded, but the few hiding in the corners, unsure of their rescuers, drifted out of the shadows and into the center of the room.

"The kids told me, men come and load them in trucks, ship them from farm to illegal farm for labor," Crankshaft said, across the back of his hand.

"And those are the lucky ones," The man with the burlap face said.

Specs ran into the barn, and when they counted heads there was a party of thirty kids—and two mysterious avengers of the night—that still needed a ride back to the city. The Bagman recognized an older boy from the gang that hung around Mac's Tobaccos, and put the older boy and Specs in charge of the other twenty children.

"How do you want to handle this?" Crankshaft said.

"If we steal a school bus, and you and I get pulled over, *we'll* be the ones doing time in Joliet. We need to call the law."

"*You're* calling the law?"

"Hey, they dress more like a taxi service than I do, and that's basically all this is. We'll take the Blue Streak to the nearest town as civilians, talk to the sheriff and the proper authorities. But we need to check on the slime first, make sure they can't ooze out of their bonds till we get back. Pile 'em in the barn?"

"Pile them in the barn," the ace mechanic and strategist said.

After they'd piled the kidnappers in their own cages, some of the kids starting pelting them with feed and manure, so Mac put Specs and the older boy in charge of making sure the other children didn't abuse their former captors, too much. The Criminal Detective and the Ace left knowing full well the kidnappers were in dangerous hands and, while they hated to admit it, part of them was still rooting for those hands.

But it wasn't as simple as all that. The nearest town, one Stafford, Indiana, population eight-hundred-and-twenty, wasn't exactly easy to find. The Sheriff had a two man office right next to the railroad track, and nowhere near town. Mac and Crankshaft used fake names. The officer there needed to call the other officer. Neither of the policemen knew where the farm was. As they approached the farm road, Mac saw another county agency with sirens and lights flaring turn down the dirt road ahead of them. Evidently, the sheriff in the next county knew where the road was.

Crankshaft turned in next to the road and pointed the two police cars behind him down the trail. Pulling back as if he were going to follow them, he spun the car toward the middle of the main road instead, hit the gas and headed north for Chicago. They flipped the switch on the Blue Streak's nitrous oxide tanks and flew out of town, more for fun that speed's sake.

Neither of them had noticed Millie Baumgartner had not been among the rescued.

●●●

A day passed and everything went back to normal, or so it seemed. But the next day, browsing through the newspaper, Mac noticed a name missing. He had been matching up the names of the kidnap victims in the paper with the names he and Crankshaft had written down, and all of them were there. But one of the victims still hadn't been found.

Millie Baumgarten had not been at the farm house. She was still missing.

The police had grilled the kidnappers for two days, and were still at it, but the slavers hadn't recognized Millie's name or her pictures. It was still on Mac's mind as he made his semi-daily rounds to the cigar store, pretending to be professional.

After greeting the clerk, Mac stuck his head out back where some boys played stickball in the alley behind the store. Morning newspapers had already sold out, but a second edition was due shortly, and most of the gang was gathered in the side alley, eager to hit the streets with a new headline to scream. Specs and Pee Wee tooled at the remnants of a chainless bicycle, balancing upside down on its seat and handles.

"Hey, Pee Wee, how are you? Specs! Heard you got kidnapped. How are you and all those other kids doing?"

"OK," Pee Wee answered for everybody.

"Yeah, it's good to be back, Mister McCullough," Specs said.

"Good to have you back," Mac said. "Hey, guys, the whole time this thing has been going on, people were looking for a few kids—and they found four times that—but there still seems to be somebody missing."

"Who?" Pee Wee said.

"Millie Baumgarten."

"Well, she wasn't out at the farm," Specs said. "Nobody there saw her and her dad's been reading the cops the riot act all day, but they don't know nothing!"

"Know '*anything*,'" Mac said.

"I already told you everything I know."

Mac continued down Spec's path of verbal sparring, apparently not minding at all. He didn't mind because it gave him a chance to keep an eye on Pee Wee, who had screwed his face up and widened his eyes at the name of Millie Baumgarten. The little kid with the blonde bangs been told not to talk about something, but his expression had shown everything. Mac watched as the six-year old tough guy edged away from the conversation, past a few boys waiting for papers and skulked toward the other end of the alley.

"Take care of yourself, Specs. See ya later," Mac said, and ambled down the alley at a pace more leisurely, yet still less time consuming, than Pee Wee's.

Mac had never tailed a six year old before. It wasn't easy.

The kid cut down the next alley toward Belmont, then cut through a vacant lot, and a hole in a fence where two slats were missing. Mac knocked three more slats out of the fence to get through it, and still tore his jacket. He came out behind a two-flat wooden home facing west, and watched as Pee Wee bopped across the backyard and up the rear stairs.

The house was a dump. More sun-bleached wood showed than paint, and what was left of the whitewash hung in patches, barely adhering to the outside of the building like lesions of respectability that hadn't quite taken. The garden looked like something out of Weird Tales Magazine, with part of a dragon's head and back sticking up through untrimmed shrubs and piles of dead, black ivy. Mac figured it was either low rent or no rent.

If the kids weren't squatting, they were paying too much.

Skirting the edges of the 'garden,' Mac slipped up the stairs, dodging a rotten hole in the porch, and stood by the rear entry. He glanced over his shoulder, down the hall and saw nobody watching. Crossing the porch, he bypassed the main rear entrance, and headed for the kitchen. Mac smelled pancakes. He stood outside and listened as young voices and the scent of flapjacks drifted through the screen door.

"Mister McCullough's askin' 'bout Millie," Pee Wee whispered in a voice so loud Mac could have heard it across the lot.

"He can keep asking," a more mature but young voice answered.

"But—but, Mister Mac's OK, Jimmy."

"Yeah, I know he's Jake with the kids and all, but nobody knows where Millie is right now. You got it?"

Mac pulled the screen door open and stood in the doorway. Jimmy, the serious boy, was flipping pancakes over the stove, while Pee Wee stood below the counter with his bangs hanging in his eyes like a blonde Shi Tzu begging for food.

"Why can't you let anybody know where she is, Jim?" Mac said.

Pee Wee's head spun toward the big man with surprise and the rarely mentioned fear of adults that only a child on his own could know. Jim ignored him, scraping the pan with a spatula.

"Look, there are a lot of things people don't talk about," Mac said, "and they should. In case you didn't know, I was one of those kids who had problems nobody talked about. I've had to hide from more than my share of adults just to become one, but now that I'm grown up, I can help. You know her family's worried about her."

"She doesn't have a family," Jimmy tossed a flapjack onto a plate Pee Wee couldn't reach. Pee Wee circled below the counter.

"Her dad's worried sick about her," the big man said.

Jimmy stopped staring at the frying pan and turned. His brows shaped an angry *V* as his eyes narrowed, and he glared at Mac.

"Her dad's worried sick about her talking," he said, pointing the spatula.

Mac considered strong-arming the kid for a second, but reconsidered. Not because he liked Jimmy, but because he knew it wouldn't work.

"Talking about what?" he asked.

"Things people don't talk about."

Something sinister crawled up the back of Mac's spine. The chill rolled his shoulders. "You think I could talk to her."

"No offense, Mister Mac, but there are things even she won't talk about."

"Look, Jimmy, a man of the world isn't offended by things. He knows they exist, and may not mention them in mixed company—but a real man does things about them when he can. Men who come up on their own—guys like you and me—we're men of the world. And we're the only ones who can help her right now." Mac glanced around the room as if for guidance. Tell me, does her father come into her room at night?"

"He touches her where he ain't s'posed to," Pee Wee said, sitting innocently at the table with his knife and fork gripped vertically in his fists.

Jimmy and Mac both glared at Pee Wee—but for different reasons.

"She upstairs?" The kids didn't answer but Mac knew. "Guys, I just need to ask her a couple of questions, just to make sure. If she doesn't want to go home, I won't make her—and, I won't mention you guys squatting in a haunted house where they forgot to turn off the gas, either."

Jimmy tore off his apron and began leading Mac through the 'living room' and upstairs. Pee Wee watched as they left the kitchen, and then glanced around the room as their footsteps faded into the distance. Climbing out of his seat, the six-year old felon checked around the corner to

"He touches her where he ain't s'posed to."

make sure nobody else was around, dragged a tin step ladder next to the stove, and began climbing toward the pancakes.

•••

By all accounts, Nathan Baumgarten appeared to be an earnest, average, American man. He had talked to the police in person this morning, and upon returning home from work to his modest bungalow off Ashland Avenue, he called them again from the telephone in his home. With his eyes closed, sitting on a seat that folded out from the wall, his arms resting on the telephone stand with his face in his hand, Nathan looked like a worried parent. He went to the kitchen and mixed himself some coffee with Canadian whiskey.

The respectable man strolled from the kitchen, gathered his newspaper and eyeglasses off the table with his other hand and sat them down next to an overstuffed chair with a footstool in front of it. Standing next to the mantle, he turned on the radio standing next to it, and tuned into a live broadcast from NBC Radio New York. Donning his horn-rim glasses, he picked up the newspaper and began tapping his feet to The Louis Armstrong Orchestra's, "Some Sweet Day."

He had a phone in his home, a radio, and imported bootleg alcohol. He was a working class hero, a success story. A respectable citizen. The man with the burlap face knew all about the facades of respectability. Like faulty building materials, they didn't stand up.

Baumgarten pulled a cigarette from a case on the half-table, and placed an ashtray on the chairs thick armrest. Reclining in his chair, he put up his feet and began to read. He'd just turned the page and spread a new set of headlines before him as Louie broke into the verse: "All my life I keep wondering where you'll be? When will I finally see the light?"

Suddenly, the radio warbled through a mix of high frequency waves and assaulted the room with sound of marching troops, announcing, "Time marches on!" Then warbled again and announced, "It's time for the WGN Barn Dance!" Fiddle music and yee-haws began vibrating the pictures on the walls. Baumgarten crumpled his newspaper, and jumped out of his chair to face the radio.

Nobody was there. Scanning every corner of the room, his hands formed fists at his sides. The respectable man sprinted into the kitchen as the radio vocalist continued to yodel about "sleeping in a hollow log." Making his way toward a cabinet drawer, Baumgarten glanced to his right and visibly jumped again.

The back door was open! He barely even used the back door. It was too early in the season to use coal for anything but cooking and he didn't drive.

The only time he opened the back door was to take out the garbage, and he hadn't done that for days. He felt a sudden chill as he tiptoed toward one of the kitchen drawers and pulled an old service revolver from it.

Shaking, Baumgarten slowly made his way back to the door, and quickly snapped the bolt closed. He checked the gun to make sure it was loaded, then went back into the living room where the voice on the radio continued to sing the praises of Texas and Tennessee. With an aggravated look on his face, the respectable man switched the radio off and scanned the room again. Crossing toward the hall, he eyed the foyer, then turned back into the living room.

He searched the entire bottom floor of the apartment, never once noticing the masked man who skulked in front of, and behind, every corner he turned. Baumgarten searched the entire house. It appeared the coast was clear.

Still glancing over his shoulders, he made his way to the desk by the rear wall. Using a key on a chain around his neck, Baumgarten opened one of the locked drawers. The revolver in one hand, he jerked the drawer open with the other. Ransacking the drawer's contents with his empty hand, his eyes and gun continued to scan the room.

He stopped a moment, thinking he had heard something, and then listened. Not even a mouse. His finger in the trigger guard, the gun hung on the back of his hand as fervent fingers pulled an envelope from the drawer and skirted through the ephemera inside, before fanning it across the table like a set of mismatched playing cards. He moaned as his fingertips continued to push the photographs around on his desk like he was trying to find just the right one for his scrapbook. Sliding an oversized picture from the pile, he leaned back in his seat and smiled to himself.

The radio roared static, full volume, then screamed from frequency to feedback. An unearthly voice wailed, "Now I got a little cabin, and it's number 44. Lord I wake up every morning, the wolf be scratching on my door!"

Baumgarten spun and leapt; his finger on the trigger. But nobody was there.

He vaulted across the room, onto the couch in front of the radio, and aimed the long barrel of his revolver over the top of it. Nobody was there.

He circled the couch and shut off the radio again.

"I know you're in here! So help me, if you don't come out, I'm going to kill you!" He said, trembling. "I know you're in here! I know it!" He was losing it. "I'll kill you!"

Aiming his gun at the shadows and silence between his own short, sharp breaths, something rattled in the kitchen behind him. Baumgarten twirled, ready to fire, then leapt through the door into the kitchen. A box of matches lay on the floor. Baumgarten pounced on it, cursing under his breath as he picked it up and turned, still scanning the room, searching all around him. A voice came out of the shadows in the living room.

"I was hoping they'd play some jailhouse songs on the Barn Dance, but I guess .44 Blues is appropriate."

Baumgarten rushed into the living room, his arm extended, and his service .38 in front of him. He saw another revolver aimed at his eye before he noticed the man behind it and froze.

"Of course, this is only a .45."

Nathan Baumgarten's revolver hung in the air at the end of his hand, but he wasn't aiming anymore. There was a moment of shock, he gasped with his mouth open, and then leaned against the door frame.

On the other side of the desk stood a man with a burlap hood wrapped tightly around his head. Blue-gray eyes burned with angry light in the shadows. The man arched his neck as if to stretch it, and the light turned to pinpoints, burning red in the sockets. In one hand the masked man held a Colt Snub Nose, in the other he held up a handful of the pictures that the respectable citizen had left spread across his desk.

"Remind me to always wait until you guys pull something out of the second drawer," The Bagman said. "Family photos?"

To Nathan Baumgarten it sounded more like a death sentence than a joke.

The respectable citizen's finger tightened on the trigger. The masked man flipped the handful of photos, backhanded at Baumgarten's face. The shot followed the cards, not the mystery man who had thrown them. As the gun went off, the Bagman vaulted over the desk, and with a strange gymnastic grace hurdled the couch to seize the abuser's wrist.

Blue eyes burned white into Baumgarten's, as each man fought with his left hand to control the gun in the other man's right. The man with the burlap face switched his grip as they struggled. He grabbed Baumgarten by the thumb of his gun hand and twisted. The respectable citizen shrunk, and his gun dropped to the floor.

"We was just playing, Mister. We was just playin'," the respectable citizen begged. "—just playing..."

The mysterious intruder hit Nathan once in the head with his .45, then holstered it beneath his lapel. Still holding Baumgarten's right wrist, the big man threw a right. Then a right, and a right, and a right—

•••

The last thing Nathan Baumgarten remembered was a leather-clad glove coming hard at his face.

The respectable man had to pry his eyelids apart to open them because

of the blood crusted in his lashes. Thinking he might be blinded, his hand
flew to his right eye, but he was almost relieved to find it had swollen shut.
He could barely see. Rolling over on his back, he ran his palm over the
lumps of his face. His head felt like one big lump beneath all the little ones.
He was both surprised and relieved to find he could move his legs. They
hadn't been broken.

At first he thought it was night, but it was actually early morning. It was
still dark, but Baumgarten could feel the dew in the air and see the lights
shimmer off Lake Michigan in the distance. Then he saw the bars breaking
the light.

Bars?

He was in jail. No, not jail—there wasn't a jail in the city a person could
see the lake from. He had to roll on one side and use his hand to sit up. He
couldn't use his stomach muscles without severe pain. Like they had all
been ripped apart.

That damned masked man. He had put him in a cage. Outside, but
where?

Clenching the hay beneath him in his hands, Baumgarten climbed to
his feet. He slipped and almost fell, but managed to stumble toward the
bars. Leaning against the iron rods imprisoning him, he wiped his mouth
with his sleeve and slowly regained his composure. There was a large pit to
his left with some sort of dead tree fixed to the ground in the middle of it.
Beyond the pit lay an unfenced plot of land, a sandy area with a few tufts of
grass and some other large pieces of tree trunks, their bark long removed
and on their last branches.

Baumgarten clenched the iron bars, spun around in a circle trying to
see through his crusty eye, and wound up with his back to them. He was in
a cage, all right. Some kind of animal cage.

He screamed for help. The word echoed back at him from across Lake
Michigan.

He yanked at the bars. Jerked with all his might, but they didn't yield.
He stumbled around, beating at the bricks, and cursed at the bolted metal
door to his left that led to the fields beyond. He was trapped. He beat on
the door with both fists and screamed until he couldn't scream anymore.
Gasping, crying through swollen eyes, he noticed a small note taped to the
top of the cage's bars.

Still using the iron rails to support himself, Baumgarten stumbled his
way to the right hand side of the cage. He had to hop a few times, almost
falling over, to finally reach the note and tear it down from where it had
been taped. He spread the parchment between his hands, and an anxious
eye ran spasmodically left to right, praying it might somehow bring him

salvation. His vision impaired, it took him a minute to understand what he had read with his swollen eye.

> Don't worry. They're only playing.
> —The Bagman

If Nathan Baumgarten had paid attention to all those newspapers he read, he would have known. The Great Depression had hit hard, and the Lincoln Park Zoo had been forced to take in animals from circuses all over the country that couldn't afford to feed them. One of those circuses had been kind enough to donate a team of tigers, several of which had turned on their original trainers. Man eaters.

Baumgarten turned his back to the bars and screamed.

It was feeding time.

The End

THE DEVIL'S SHINGLE

A Crankshaft Solo Adventure

Antoine "Crankshaft" Jones was not the kind of guy who stayed home on Saturday Nights. Crankshaft worked hard. He not only put in sixty hours a week at work, but spent a good deal of the rest of his time trying to keep his friend Mac McCullough, The Bagman, from not going completely berserk. Only a handful of people knew that Crankshaft was also the "Martian" in coveralls and reflective goggles that assisted the masked avenger, and Crank had to spend a lot of his time covering that up. So at the end of the week, the ace mechanic sought a release. And Maxwell Street, on Chicago's near-west side, was the place that gave him that release.

Being a night owl by nature, the Maxwell Street scene was perfect for the Chicago artist of the automobile. After listening to the Blues all night, Crankshaft would have a big breakfast and shop at the Maxwell Street Market the next morning. But the night—which really didn't start until the early hours of the morning—always started at "The Gates." The Gates started as a speakeasy during prohibition, but had since turned into an almost legitimate nightclub—despite really just being a speakeasy disguised as a Blues Club.

"Damn, Ol' Jellyroll's been drinking something bonded," Crank's buddy, Tampa Slim said.

"Sounds like he finally found a way to wrap his chubby fingers around a guitar string," the ace mechanic yelled over the music across the table. "He's gotten better since the last time I saw him play."

The fat man onstage, Jellyroll Jake Hawkins, rattled off a guitar riff that struck like a snake then blended back into the rhythm section like he'd been there all along.

"Better? The boy's playing rhythm and lead *at the same time!*" Tampa Slim tapped his cigar on the ashtray. "He couldn't play two strings last time I saw him, and now he's playing like two bands at once!"

As if to emphasize Silk's point, Jellyroll stuck five notes into the dialogue between beats. His National Steel Guitar shook the walls as it led the back-beat one moment, only to slide into a steely-toned lead the next. The last three chords blended into one note that seemed to fill the air as the "Resonator Guitar" lived up to its name. Smoke pushed its way down from the ceiling as the notes dissolved in the air, and the crowd applauded the end of the set. The band announced a fifteen minute intermission.

The crowd cheered. They whistled, they howled, hooted and hollered, and then ordered a round for the band, too. The musicians circled from stage, to backstage, and to the bar in a procession. The crowd surrounded them. Jellyroll Hawkins was a hit.

"Weird, huh?" Tampa Slim said, sipping whiskey from a coffee cup. "From ugly duckling to mockingbird overnight. It seems Jellyroll's been taking some lessons."

"And copious notes, too." Crankshaft said. "Maybe all that time he spent playing out on the street finally kicked some fuel into the carburetor."

"Must've just hit the fuel tank, 'cause last week it looked like he was try-ing to learn how to play a G-chord."

"Sometimes it works that way," the ace mechanic said. "You have to watch the wheels go round a few times before you know where all the cogs fit. Then, usually when you least expect it, everything kind of fits together in a big picture in your head."

"Yeah, if you got a head full of cogs and gears."

"No, with just about anything. You see it done. You try to do it. You stink. You watch how other people do it, but you keep trying. Then one day it just kicks in, and you've got it. I don't know what Hawkins has been doing—but he *got* the Blues."

"Or it got him. 'Cause last week he was all set to stink for a couple more years."

"What about that Sonny Boy, kid? The one that plays the harmonica. All he did was honk on that thing for two years, then one day, next thing you know, he's created a whole new sound."

"Yeah, but Sonny Boy accidentally swallowed the whole damn Blues harp. If he hadn't learned to play fast, he would've suffocated." Tampa Slim watched the band members stroll backstage with their coffee cups cam-ouflaging the bottom shelf liquor. "I'm not even sure he would've started playing it, if he hadn't seen 'ol Shimmy Wilson soaking his harmonica in a glassful full of vodka."

"Easy to believe, but—"

"But nothing," Tampa said, upending his cup. "Something shady's going on with Hawkins."

"'Something shady'?" Crankshaft said. "Do I have to start calling him Slick Shady Jellyroll now? Because I don't think I can do that."

"No, not Slick Shady." Tampa waved a finger in front of him. "But shady, something's just-not-right."

"Sounds a little like jealousy to me."

"Please, son, back in my day—" Before Tampa Slim had a chance to fin-ish somebody screamed bloody murder from the back room.

"Oh, my God, oh my God, oh my God!" a woman yelled. "Somebody killed Jake!"

"Get her out of here!" a man's voice said backstage. "Somebody get the club owner—and don't let any more women out there. His head's punched in."

Without thinking, Crankshaft realized he was already across the room and headed backstage to investigate. Nevertheless, his buddy, Tampa Slim was right behind him, hat and cane in hand.

"What happened?" Crankshaft eyed the bouncer at the back door.

The man recognized Crank and shoved the door open, revealing Jellyroll's body in the alley just beyond it. Several band members and club employees stood over the corpse.

Crankshaft stepped between two of the men and saw Jellyroll lying peacefully on the ground. There was no blood, no sign of a fight. He felt beneath Jellyroll's chins for his pulse. There was no pulse, either. A man on the other side of the body held Jellyroll's hair and pointed at the back of the dead man's skull.

"Must've fallen down and hit his head," a younger guitar player said.

"And killed himself? Like that?" Tampa Slim said. "Please, that kid's got a skull like a fire hydrant. It'd take a monkey wrench to dent the thing!"

"Maybe he slipped and fell," somebody else said.

"On what, kid?" Tampa picked up a handful of sand from the alleyway. "Ain't rained in weeks and nobody's been changing oil back here."

"You don't think—" another man said.

"Something shady is what I think," Tampa answered.

"But his wallet's still on him, for whatever that's worth." The man glanced inside the folded leather and shook it in the air. "Not much, evidently."

Two barrel-shaped bouncers pushed their way through the small crowd and stood guard over the body as a gruff, but feminine, voice announced through the backstage door.

"You men know if the cops find that body near The Gates, they'll close me down in a heartbeat," Ruby, The Gates manager said, leaning outside the door and staring at the men. "If you want to call the police, you can, but you found him on the next block."

"No, no cops," a couple of members of the band said. A bouncer and two other men nodded in agreement, Crankshaft included. Of course he had his own reasons, but Crank had no doubt some of the musicians might have warrants out for their arrest. Blues musicians were a strange crowd, and a lot of them changed their names for reasons other than wanting to add a verb to their signature.

"Hold it," Crankshaft said.

Considering the size of Ruby and her bouncers, everybody else looked at the ace mechanic like he was crazy. But a man toward the back of the crowd began to fade down the alley. Crankshaft pounced from where he stood, grabbing him by the shoulder and stopping him cold. The man turned to brush off Crankshaft's hand. Crankshaft gripped him tighter, shook the man, and held up his other hand as if to slap to him.

"Everybody here know everybody else?" Crank was reticent about coming right out and asking for names, but he wanted to find out what had happened, and to do that he needed to know who was involved. Tampa Slim understood immediately.

"I know just about everybody here, Crank, except for the employees." He held his walking stick up in front of the club's bouncers. "That's Petey Wheatstraw you got your hand on. The other guitar player's Bobby." He pointed the rest of the men out individually by way of introduction. "Kokomo, you may know as Gitfiddle Jim, Willie on bass, and Stax Stephens on drumsticks." He pointed out the last member, a man with a harmonica wedged into the side of his jaw like a chaw of tobacco. "And I believe we both know Sonny Boy."

Sonny blew the first four notes of "I'm a Man" without touching the blues harp in his mouth, declaring his status. Crankshaft rolled his eyes. At least with the Bagman, Crank knew which shifty characters were on his side. Then he realized, none of them ever were, and he was right back where he'd started. The ace mechanic leaned toward Tampa and whispered.

"These guys all have pretty regular gigs around here? I mean, I know Willie and Sonny Boy do, but I don't know anything about the others."

"Kokomo works at a steel mill just outside town. Stax and Bobby been touring regular for a few years. Bobby's been here maybe six-months, but that's nothing new. And Petey Wheatstraw ain't going nowhere. Far as I can tell, the men that might leave would have to come back for work."

Crankshaft nodded. Bluesmen always came back to Maxwell Street for quick cash. He knelt down one last time to take a look at the back of Jellyroll's head then stood back up. Without a word, a car backed down the alley. Ruby's bodyguard's picked up Jellyroll by the hands and feet and threw him in the trunk.

"Waitaminute, we can't just all walk off like nothing happened," Bobby the guitar player said.

"He's right," Tampa Slim said. "Even the cops would *pretend* to do something. We can't just let somebody start murdering musicians and walking away." Several of the others began to nod along and murmur. Crankshaft noticed the early morning sun rising like an orange ball over Roosevelt Road.

"Who wants breakfast? I'll buy—if it's under two-bits," Crankshaft said. Food would be cheaper when the Market opened in an hour, but he knew it was the only way to keep the group together.

Sonny Boy spat out his harmonica and joined in with Crankshaft, Tampa and the musicians. Petey Wheatstraw backed away, slowly at first, and then hustled off as if he wanted to break into a run.

"What's wrong with him?" Crankshaft said.

"Petey's kinda slow," Tampa Slim said. "Baptists down the block take care of him, but they don't know he's camped out behind The Gates every night listening to the music. I suppose he doesn't like the idea of having to lie to the preachers about where he's been. That and the poor kid raised himself on the street."

"Petey's got trust problems," Bobby the guitar player said. "He don't trust anybody, and for all the right reasons."

●●●

Crankshaft shrugged his shoulders and the merry band made their way around the corner to Dinah's Diner, where Crank ordered the "two egg and coffee special" for everybody. It took a while before the conversation got back to murder again. It was obvious to the ace mechanic that Jellyroll couldn't have been too popular given the reaction of his bandmates. But what he really needed was a list of enemies.

"So how did you guys know Jellyroll?" he asked.

"Not good enough to ask for that steel guitar of his," Bobby said. "I been in Chicago almost six-months now, and never even noticed him till maybe three weeks ago. I was kind of amazed I hadn't noticed somebody who could play like that before."

"Same here," Willie the bass player said and pointed with his fork across the table at Sonny Boy. "Sonny and I grew up around here, and the only other time I noticed Jellyroll was when he played in front of the Men's Store. His fills came in late, and he couldn't strum a melody to save his life. Guess he's been practicin'."

Tampa Slim shook his head as if he couldn't believe it. Everybody but Crankshaft kept eating as they shrugged and nodded.

"So nobody even knows this guy enough to want to kill him," Crankshaft said. The musicians answered by shrugging some more while they ate. "What about the woman that screamed his name from the backroom?"

"Oda Jeffries?" Sonny Boy said, through a mouthful of toast and eggs. "She was going out with Harry Watson, come to think of it. But, she's Oda Jeffries. It's Saturday night, the crowds thinning out, and Oda knows she's getting better looking to every man in the bar by the drink." He turned and winked at Crankshaft. "Oda does not like to go home alone. It's possible—maybe. But let's face it; Jellyroll was the man of the hour. Of course, she'd be trying to hook him in."

"Harry Watson?" Crankshaft made a mental note.

"Last week's man of the hour," Bobby said.

"Another guitar player?" Crank said.

The rest of the group nodded as one.

"Maybe it *was* an accident," Kokomo said.

"You tell me, Mr. Ironworker," Tampa Slim said. "You think a buffalo of a man like Jellyroll just fell down and caved his own skull in?"

"No," Kokomo muttered. The musicians all shook their heads in agreement.

"Then why would somebody kill him?" Crankshaft said. "Sex? Money? Power?"

"Jellyroll had none of those things," Sonny Boy said.

"So what did he have that somebody would kill him for?"

Everybody shook their heads and shrugged their shoulders.

●●●

After Crankshaft paid the check, most of the musicians left to pick their equipment up, so they could play on the street for the Sunday Morning Market. Tampa Slim noticed Crankshaft staring into the space in front of him as they made their way back toward Maxwell Street.

"What's the matter?"

"There's no motive," the mechanic answered. "Jellyroll might as well have been a street lamp where these people were concerned. The only reason they even knew him was his ability to play guitar. He didn't have anything worth killing for."

"He had the Blues," Tampa Slim said.

"You can't really steal that," Crankshaft said.

"You know, my old friend, Bluesmen are a fearful and superstitious lot. I know because I'm one of them."

"So?"

"'So?' Think like a Bluesman. And remember, he had a *new-found* ability to play the guitar."

"You saying he was haunted? I don't think that's a real motive."

"Not if you think of it that way. But remember what you were asking about—money, romance, and power. Not much money, yet. Sex, but no romance— That leaves power." Tampa Slim took off his boater and brushed his bushy red hair down. Pulling the straw hats brim down low, he spoke across the back of his hand. "Did you notice me going through Jellyroll's pockets with that other guy, so I could make sure he wasn't trying to hide anything?"

"I was making sure *you* weren't trying to hide anything."

"Well, I got to be honest." He looked both ways. "I was looking for something."

"What?"

"Jellyroll's guitar-pick, it wasn't there. Did you see it when he was playing at the club?" Tampa held his cane like a guitar and strummed it as they idled up the middle of the street. "Thing was made out of stone and hooked around his finger, had a picture of some of big-headed goon carved on the wraparound part. I've only seen one guy use a guitar-pick like that in my life, and he was good, but not that good. And, I've never seen one that wrapped around a man's finger."

"Are you saying somebody murdered him for a guitar pick?" Crankshaft said.

"A strange, *new* guitar-pick," Tampa answered. "Or a very, very old one."

"Now you're just talking about Voodoo."

"Maybe, but Bluesmen *are* a superstitious lot." Tampa pointed at a line of them setting up stage in front of stores on the street. "And a lot of them think alike. Catch you later. I'm going to find some shade to sit and play in. Maybe make a few dollars."

Crankshaft waved and headed the other direction. Somebody next to a brick wall in an alley strangled the string of a steel-guitar, the wailing metal-wound strings unintentionally announcing the opening of the Sunday Street Market. Trucks and merchants had been stocking their wares on the open lot from Halsted to 16th Street for hours, and reacted to the first blast of sound as if it were the starting shot of a footrace. Maxwell Street, the Ellis Island of the Midwest, the largest open-air market in America, was now open for business.

One could get anything at the Maxwell Street Market, legal or illegal. Few questions were asked about where the stuff came from, and everybody knew a good deal of the merchandise had possibly "fallen off the truck." Meanwhile, foreign wholesalers lined the street with imports from all over the world. Smart vendors marked it up a hundred percent and still beat store prices. Then, the local retailers learned that bands outside brought business inside, and an American phenomenon had been born. The Maxwell Street Market, the only place in America honest enough to promise they would "Cheat you fair!"

And with the Police Academy next door, while the mob "saved spaces" for the vendors in the street, nothing could have been more typically Chicago. Between pick-up trucks, mule carts, automobiles, shipping vans, horse buggies and carriages, there wasn't a parking space for blocks. And every one of those vehicles—all with their doors open—were buying, selling, or trading something.

Distracted by the action, Crankshaft scoured the tool vendors whose wares lay on tables and blankets over a half acre lot. He made his way through the piles of carving instruments, some new electric-powered tools, and some completely powerless tools. The kind you had to plug in and make sure they worked before you closed a deal.

"Mornin' everybody! My names Harry Watson!" a voice yelled from across the street. A guitar slammed four chords and the voice began to sing. "I go-o-ot the blues!"

Harry Watson. Oda Jeffries "man of the hour" last week. Crankshaft stepped under the awning of a clothing store and leaned against the brick building to watch. Then he realized, if Harry Watson was playing this early at the Market, he probably had a gig last night. And an alibi.

Somebody in the crowd yelled, "Harry, you are truly THE midnight to six man!" and toasted him with a flask. Crankshaft asked the man and was told the crowd had followed Watson from Eight Hundred Des Plaines—some clubs had only addresses, no names—where Watson had been playing the night before.

Five minutes later, a woman in an evening dress—much too revealing for her to be on her way to church—stood up next to the band between songs. The woman gave Harry a hug and a kiss and sat down almost next to him, crossing her legs and glancing up with adoring eyes as she cupped her palms over one knee. Even if he hadn't had an alibi, Harry certainly didn't look like the jealous type.

Crankshaft scoffed, and then made his way back into crowd, past an old Mexican woman selling fruits and vegetables, before he thought of solving the murder again. He bought four *pablano* peppers and as the saleswoman put them in a bag, he ran the seven deadly sins through his head again, searching for a motive.

Greed? The only thing Jellyroll had of value was his guitar, and nobody was trying to take it. Anger? Nobody seemed to know the victim enough to be all that angry at him. Gluttony was out. Lust? Again, nobody seemed to care enough. Then he hit sloth, pride, and envy.

Damned if Tampa Slim's theory was the only one that worked. He had to think like a Bluesman. If there was some sort of magical talisman that made men into musical wizards—a pretty big "If" in Crank's point of view—then gaining that magic was all about power. Sloth, pride, and envy may have been the motive, but power appealed to an entire grocery list of deadly sins.

Crankshaft hated Voodoo. He was a man of science. Hard science. Physics, patterns, engineering, applied mechanics, these were his specialty. He knew human behavior and psychology, but that was really the Bagman's specialty. Mac could step into other people's heads in an instant, but Crank had always figured that was because most of the time he was trying to figure where is own head was."

From Crank's point of view, there were too many things in the real world to be afraid of without bringing the supernatural into it. If he'd learned nothing else working with the Bagman, it was that monsters didn't hide in the closet or under the bed—they sat right across the table from you. Sometimes they even turned out to be your family and friends.

He needed more information about unnatural things.

Applying his newfound Bluesman's thought process, he decided to find a fortune teller. Just sticking his head up, he could see two palm-readers, a card reader, and a spiritualist. He rolled his eyes and sighed again. There was no way in hell he was going to pay for information about the supernatural. By definition, it didn't make sense. It was like buying an encyclopedia full of stuff you wanted to read instead of facts. He simply could not get himself to do it. He just couldn't see that crowd *cheating him fair.*"

Turning around, the Ace from Addison Street headed into a small swarm of music vendors near a Maxwell Street Polish Sandwich stand. An old man in back of one of the booths had a Victrola wound up to play '78 records and the recorded versions of the sheet music he was selling. The white-bearded gent sat in a chair leaning against the home of the "The Maxwell Street Polish." Fanning away the heat and grilled onion humidity with a song book, the old man tapped his foot in front of him as he listened to a Texas Swing tune called The Hamburger Hop.

"You sell those instruments, too?" Crankshaft waved at the table next the old man.

"From Blues harps to Jews Harps, brass horns to ass horns; strings to skins to Hillbilly Guitars." The old man said. "Records and sheet music, too," he added in a separate announcer's voice then spat into the sand.

"How you doing, Duke?" Crankshaft said.

Duke wasn't the man's real name. Neither was Maxwell, but that's what everybody knew him as: Duke Maxwell, Duke's Maxwell Street Music. Nobody knew Duke's real name. Nobody knew where he was from. He'd either appeared years ago and nobody noticed, or he had just always been there. For all the evidence, he could have crawled out from beneath the street. He was The Duke of Maxwell Street.

"What about guitar picks?"

"Three for a dime. Heavy, medium, or light?"

"Thumb-picks."

"Fifteen cents and up, depending on what you're looking for."

"I'm looking for a particular style of thumb-pick, Duke." Crankshaft

"How you doing, Duke?" Crankshaft said.

pulled a five dollar bill out of his pocket and stuck it in front of the old man's overalls. "This one's made out of stone."

"I deal in musical instruments and lessons, Mr. Race Car Driver." The Duke lowered the front legs of his chair to the ground and pointed at Crankshaft with his pipe. "Not Bullfinch's Mythology—and *certainly not* anything so evil as to threaten the relationship between Man, Blues, and 'God-kind.'"

Crankshaft smiled. He'd paid the right person. *Cheat you fair!*

"So you know the guitar-pick I'm looking for? Made out of stone and has a carving of a man, or something, with a big head on the thumb part?"

"That ain't no man, and there ain't no good come to anybody looking for that guitar pick," Duke said. He pulled the money out of his overall's bib and began to stick it back it the mechanic's shirt. Crankshaft brushed the old man's hand away.

"I'm not looking for the pick, just information. I want to know the story behind it. I think it may have gotten somebody killed."

"Nothing new about that. That pick is cursed," Duke said, sticking the bill back in his overalls. "Legend has it, that it was carved out of a blood-stone, found in the middle of the crossroads by an insane Bluesman who sold his soul to the devil on that very spot. Story first came out of Mississippi—probably before the Civil War, but before I was born, and I'm downright prehistoric!" The old man winked and eyed his display tables as he leaned back and continued.

"That big-headed critter carved on it is a Mayan Death God. See, when that Bluesman pulled the stone out of the ground, the stories say it up and bit him, grabbed hold, and curled round his finger like a King Snake. The old men by the bayou used to call it 'The Devil's Shingle' back where I grew up. Satan himself was supposed to have burned some sort of demon into it. 'Course, the legend is that the Devil's Shingle is a gift that comes with a curse. Give it to anybody, not just guitar players, and everybody—anybody—can play along with the music of the spheres. The stories always seem to involve guitar players, though."

"So, anybody gets a hold of this thing, keyboard player, drummer, violinist, he's supposed to become incredible?"

"Exactly, they'll have the gift. But what the Bluesman don't know is, the waves and melodies of the universe, they got to balance. Before long, those soulful rhythms turn short and sharp. And the melodies turn dark. The Blues is about living with darkness, laughing at it—not being part of it. Take away that balance, and you got nothing but funeral dirges and requiems."

"What happens to them?" Crankshaft picked up one of the thumb picks and began to examine it. "I mean, how does the curse work?"

"What happens to 'em?" The Duke slapped his knee and laughed. "They get everything they want! That's what usually kills 'em. Then they find out they don't want nothin'. Not even their own so-called friends and family can stop the Shingle. So, besides everybody else trying to kill 'em for the Devil's pick, anybody that ever *cared about* 'em feels cheated. Lovers stray and families resent. Business partners might as well be talkin' to a morphine addict. Don't nothing matter but the music. And as a man pulls away from humanity the rhythm drags and all the chords come out in minor keys. It ain't music anymore. It's just pain. " The old man paused a second, sipped from his lemonade and stared into the throngs of people like he was looking at the clouds. "'Course, most of 'em die before that—or just disappear."

"You wouldn't have happened to see anybody trying to sell a pick like that, would you?"

"Only someone truly blessed could ever let that thing go. Regular people, the Devil's Shingle takes over. Don't matter if you're a saint, a sinner, a child or an immortal. Man's got to have a special bond with his maker to hand that little trinket around."

Crankshaft wrapped his hand around his jaw in thought. The Duke's eyes glimmered with sudden insight.

"You're looking for somebody who stole it, ain't ya?" the old man said.

"I'm looking for somebody who killed somebody to get it," the ace mechanic answered.

"All you got to do is wait and listen. Whoever picked up the Shingle will be off the street and playing the clubs in a week. Heck, they'll prob'ly be recording and playing on Broadway in New York—then they'll be in the gutter."

"And nobody will care." Crankshaft kept staring into space. "So how can I find this man before the Devil's Shingle steals his soul?"

"Logic?" Duke laughed as he said it. "But remember, the Devil's Blues don't make no sense."

Great, so he was back to thinking like a Bluesman. Crankshaft thanked the Duke, walked across the street and ordered a cup of coffee at a rickety wooden stand somebody had probably nailed together where it stood. He was tired, but the mystery was eating at him.

Watching the crowd without leaning against the stand, a herd of some thirty people came hurtling down the street, dodging between marketers, and pushing through the crowd.

Four chords climbed from E to A and back then echoed down the block. It was like a question waiting for a response, and the entire crowd turned to answer. Big Bill Broonzy had run a plug from a barber shop and was playing an *electric* guitar! Crankshaft had seen the Frying Pan variety and not been too impressed, but Big Bill had modified some kind of acoustic. It had neither the raw edge of the Resonator or the tinny sound of the Frying Pan. The notes filled the air with a mixture of twang and fuzz that created its own texture.

Crankshaft's head spun around on his shoulders. He'd never heard anything like it. Downing most of his coffee and pouring the rest into the sand lot, he slowly made his way up through the crowd, squeezing along the edge of the street. Broonzy had launched the crowd into a frenzy. And Big Bill had been around the club last night. Crankshaft stuck his head between the feathers on two women's hats to look. *Could Big Bill have the—?*

"Damnit," Crank cursed out loud. Broonzy's new sound had nothing to do with the pick. He was playing with his fingers.

The women in front of him turned around, one of them apparently offended, the other laughing. Crankshaft nodded his head in apology and slid back into the crowd.

He couldn't do this just thinking like a Bluesman, he had to use logic, or at least a Bluesman's logic; whatever that was. Once again, he went through the night before in his head. And that's when it him.

Jellyroll Hawkins had just left the stage last night, ordered a drink, stopped to talk to Oda at the back door, and stepped outside. Then the band went out to get some air and found him. Unless everybody in the band was in on it—and they weren't—that left only one suspect.

Petey Wheatstraw. The slow boy who sat in the alley listening to Blues through the door all night.

Crankshaft looked at his watch. It was after noon. Church would be out. And Petey Wheatstraw would most likely be at the Baptist Church that helped take care of him. The mechanic straightened his tie and decided to get some religion.

•••

With a name like The First Baptist Church of Southeast Chicago it may have sounded like the ministry was trying to squeeze into a neighborhood, but the fact was the First Baptist had been there when the Southeast side was just Southside, since before the Civil War. The majority of churches and temples near the market were of Eastern European origin now, but the First Baptist stood proudly. As old and as it was, the church had sprung up from the same soil that nurtured the first settlers and the first Bluesmen.

From the corner, Crank could see the gospel choir's musicians filing out onto the street with their instrument cases in their hands. The First Baptist had the best Gospel band in the city, and many were the Blues musicians who turned down Maxwell Street's early morning gigs just to have the hon-

or of playing with the choir. Pastor Richard Noble, a neighborhood fixture, stood outside shaking hands. Watching the rest of the congregation gather in the courtyard, Crankshaft spotted Petey Wheatstraw bypassing the rest of the crowd, carrying a ukulele toward a gang of children playing around a rope-swing. After a moment of serious consideration, Crankshaft thought it might be better to talk to Pastor Richie first. After the crowd thinned, Crankshaft approached Pastor Richie and introduced himself.

"Crankshaft Jones?" the Pastor said. "Pleasure to meet you. Saw you race back in the day."

"The pleasure's all mine, sir. This was the first church I ever set foot in when I got to Chicago. Um, I was wondering, if maybe I might be able to talk to Petey Wheatstraw."

"What about?" Pastor Richie seemed suddenly protective.

"There was a robbery last night, and I think Petey may have been a witness." Crankshaft felt it best to leave the words "murder" and "suspect" out of his request, or the answer would be "no."

"Behind The Gates, huh?"

"Yeah. I guess news must travel fast around here."

"Not that fast. Petey practically lives back there. We keep telling him he's going to get in trouble, but he the only thing he listens to is music—and, maybe, the *occasional* prayer. You do know he's slow, right?"

"That's what I heard."

"Well, it's not stupidity. He's smart about a lot of things. It's just because of the way his mind works, and the way he brought himself up. He gets mixed up sometimes, overemotional. Of course, he'd never admit to hanging around a Blues club in front of me or the staff, so you'll be on your own."

"Thank you," Crankshaft said. "I appreciate your trust."

"Trust nothing." Pastor Richie grabbed him by the arm. "You so much as mess a hair on that boy's head, I'll sic the whole Church choir on you. Al Capone couldn't stand up to a gang of old women who think Blues is the devil's music." He smiled then added threateningly, "And, I'll be the one telling them *you* gave him the Blues."

"Uh, thanks?" Crankshaft wasn't too sure what to think. It didn't sound like Pastor Richie thought the Blues was evil, but it sounded like he knew how to rile up a crowd.

The pastor put two fingers in his mouth, whistled across the lot, and waved for Petey Wheatstraw to come over. Petey grabbed his ukulele and began sprinting across the lot, until he spotted Crankshaft then glanced around and slowed to shuffle.

"Petey, this is Crankshaft Jones," Pastor Richie said. "He'd like to talk to you about something you may have seen last night."

Billie looked at Crankshaft like the mechanic had ratted him out.

"I'll leave you to discuss this between yourselves. I'll be inside if you need anything, Petey." He nodded his head at the both of them as Petey handed him the ukulele for safekeeping. "Nice meeting you, Mr. Jones."

"Hi, Petey." Crankshaft shoved his hat back in an effort to look friendly and smiled. "Your name really Petey Wheatstraw?"

"You know it's not," he said blankly. "I'm not stupid mister, I just get confused sometimes." He shifted in his seat again. "And I know why you're here."

"Well, I'm glad *you* do, because I'm not completely sure myself." Crankshaft shook some cigarettes out the end of a pack of Camels and offered Petey one. Wheatstraw made a stop sign with his hand.

"Mizz Applebee'd be swatting me, if she saw me smoking, Mr. Crankshaft." He glanced over his shoulders as if he were being watched. "Can you do me a favor?"

"What?"

"I'll tell you whatever you want to know. I'll even tell the police. But please," he clenched his cap in his hands in front of his chest, "can we go somewhere else? I don't want Mizz Applebee to find out I was outside The Gates again. She gets really angry. Pastor Richie gets it, but the Baptist women all think it's the devil's music."

Crankshaft suddenly understood that Wheatstraw was more worried about what the people at church thought than the law.

"Sure, sure. OK if we head back to Maxwell Street?"

"As long as we don't go all the way there. I'll get in trouble."

"Tell you what," Crankshaft pointed across the street. "Why don't we just stop there for some ice cream? That OK with you? I'll buy?"

"I love ice cream as much as God, almost," Petey said with a childlike seriousness.

Inside the Ice Cream Parlor, Crankshaft got pistachio, and Petey ordered a chocolate cone. After sitting down and watching the traffic outside the window, Petey was still trying to lick the chocolate from dripping on his hand when Crankshaft tried to get to the matter at hand.

"You like the Blues, too? Don't you, Petey?"

Petey jumped in his seat. His feet fluttered under the table like he wanted to get up but was afraid to. He wound up squirming on the back corner of his chair. He never answered, just stared.

"I'm not passing judgment, Petey. I like the Blues, too. God works in mysterious ways, and he says we should sing and play. He never said what kind of songs."

Petey wiggled in his seat.

"I won't tell the church ladies anything, Petey."

Petey buried his face in his hands and collapsed onto the table bawling. After a few minutes, Crankshaft stood up, wrapped an arm around the man-child and led him outside. Petey was still crying as they walked around the corner and into an alley. The same alley where they had been the night before.

Petey wailed awhile then snuffled, his tears seeming to free him. He looked up at Crankshaft for the first time with something like human kinship in his eyes.

"I didn't mean to kill him! I didn't! It was an accident, Mr. Crankshaft!" He bawled.

Crankshaft held the man in his arms. Petey cried on his shoulder.

"I—I didn't mean to. It was an accident. I just didn't want Jellyroll to go to hell!"

"You didn't want Jellyroll going to hell?" Crankshaft lowered Petey to the ground and sat down next to him. "What made you think he was going to hell?"

"Bobby said he was. Bobby said the devil gave Mr. Hawkins a piece of his horns. I liked Jellyroll. He was funny—till he got a piece of that ol' devil horn. Then he stopped talkin' to me, stopped talking to anybody at all. Bobby said if I didn't get that horn away from Jellyroll, that he'd go to hell!"

"So you tried to steal it from him?"

"I never stole anything before in my life, Mr. Crankshaft. I never will again—but I had to. I didn't mean to kill him. I just meant to knock him out!" Petey gasped, catching his breath between sobs. "I just didn't want him going to hell."

Crankshaft held Petey by the shoulders. It was hard for him to believe a man so strong could be so fragile. But Petey was scared. And living in a world he didn't understand made everything even scarier. The last thing Crankshaft wanted to do was shut down his world. And cutting Wheatstraw away from the musical comfort he had found in the Blues might just cut him off forever.

"Did you give that 'devil's horn' to Bobby?"

"I had to Mr. Crankshaft. He said anybody that kept it would go straight to hell!"

"Yeah— I bet he did." Bobby the guitar player had set him up and poor Petey didn't even know it, probably still trusted him. "'*Trust problems*' my ass," Crankshaft thought, remembering what Bobby had said. The kind of trust Petey had meant something—even in this world. Something like that took a certain kind of innocence, something the middle-aged mechanic had never had.

Then Crankshaft remembered what the Duke of Maxwell Street had told him about the Devil's Shingle. "*Only someone truly blessed could ever let that thing go. Regular people, the Devil's Shingle takes over—Man's got to have a special bond with his maker to hand that little trinket around."* He stared at the space in front of him for a moment, thinking.

"Listen, Petey, you know nobody on earth knows God's real will, right? God's will, not mankind's? This world's too big for a man to control. All he can do is keep his side of the street clean, right? Jellyroll was turning mean, like some dogs do. Now, I'm not saying he should've been handled like a mad dog, but, the way fate works, something bad was bound to happen. What happened shouldn't have, and I'm going to count on you not to let it happen again. But Bobby used you to do something bad. I want you to stay away from him." Crankshaft stood the man up again, dusted him off and continued.

"Petey, if I can forgive you, God and the universe sure as hell can, too. I want you to go back to the home and forgive yourself. This is just between you, me, and the Big Guy," Crankshaft pointed at all three, then thumbed at his chest. "I'm not going to tell a soul, because I don't think you meant to do anything wrong. Be at peace, kid. See ya in church next week, OK?" Crankshaft hesitated a moment, thinking of his own particular brand of peace. "Nah, tell you what, Saturday night behind The Gates. I'll be there."

"What about Bobby?"

"You let me take care of Bobby."

•••

It had taken Crankshaft the rest of the afternoon asking around the market to find out Bobby's real name. He didn't need it. Instead he went back to the strip Monday night. Then Tuesday. Wednesday night he heard it. A sound wafted in on the ragweed like a germ in the wind, and a melody filled the night air with a steady, rhythmic beat. A trolley car rang in the background, but even as the sound drowned out the guitar, its player hooked a riff around the city noise. Like a fire in the distance, those who heard it were compelled to investigate.

Crankshaft leaned back, stuck his hands in his pockets and listened for a moment, then stepped into the murk between the faded circles of light beneath the two lampposts on Newberry Street. Heading in the direction of the music, he could see a few people with their hands cupped above their eyes trying to peek into the window of the 1313. Another club with an address instead of a name. It wasn't too bad for a dive.

"All the place needs is plumbing and electricity," Crankshaft thought and went inside. There were maybe thirty people in the club, a good crowd for such a small place, especially since it was still early in the week. Crankshaft stood left of the door as his eyes adjusted to the darkness across from the solitary stage light in back of the club. When the blur of lighting behind the bar transformed into promotional neon, he he entered, and ordered a double Scotch. Black Label. Top Shelf.

Crankshaft was a notorious penny-pincher. After the war he'd come home a hero from France, only to find he was just another black man in America. Times had been tough, and it was rare that his stoic personality allowed him to think of celebrating almost anything. He preferred to think it was because he was more than grateful for what he had, but the fact was, he was a cheapskate.

So it looked even odder when the man with the driving goggles propped on the bill of his cap melted into the shadows and popped back up lighting a match to a Cuban cigar in the darkest corner of the room. He puffed, slowly, held his mouth open tasting the smoke and sipped on the finest Scotch Chicago's Irish could muster. The band went into the next number.

Crossing his legs, the ace mechanic stared at his drink as if coming to some sort of decision. He puffed on his cigar leaned back and watched the crowd listening to the music.

They soon broke into dance. Crankshaft didn't listen, so much as hear. He didn't realize it, but it was the same thing he'd done in the Great War, mentally blocking out the background noise of the enemy's barrage so he could deal with the problem at hand. By the time the music had stopped and started three more times, the tiny crowd waved like a sea awash. Heads and arms popped out around the fringes as dancers twirled their partners, twisting and flipping through the air. Crankshaft sat back in the darkness, sipping his drink until last call. It was four A.M. There were still about ten people left in the club.

With most of the crowd on the south side of sober, the band made no closing announcement and improvised for a while. The bass player twirled his instrument and broke into a solo, bouncing off two different scales. The guitar player shot a note in-between. It was perfect, better than if it had been rehearsed. They played the chorus one more time, and the bartender kicked everybody out. "You don't have to go home, but you can't stay here!"

When he said it, Crankshaft was already in the back room. The Bagman had never taught the mechanic how to pick a lock, and Crank didn't want to know. So he'd simply stuck the handle of a sawed-off, bolt cutter in the armpit of his jacket and waited for the last, and loudest, chorus of the show. When the band hit the crescendo, Crank chopped the padlock to the stockroom open and went inside. Examining the liquor stock on the wall, he neither drank nor smoked as he listened to the crowd leaving. He heard the bartender putting chairs on the tables, and footsteps approaching the stockroom door.

The latch on the other side rattled as the bartender wiggled it, apparently wondering where the padlock had gone. The door swung open, and stuck on the swollen hardwood of the barroom floor. The bartender stared at Crankshaft a second, surprised, his head beginning to tilt to the side. A calloused black hand yanked the barman inside by the wrist and slung him into the shadows. The door slid closed behind him.

Bobby and the boys in the band were packing up their instruments and equipment, getting ready to get paid. While a guitar player gently looped the band's only electrical cord into a lasso, Bobby had broken down the microphone stand and was already leaning against its shortened staff like a cane as he sat down at the bar. After a few minutes, he walked around the bar and started pouring beer into mugs for the band as they gathered around.

Crankshaft slid out of the stockroom door, and stuck the broken padlock back into the latch. Stepping out of the gloom, he poured himself a beer then sat down next to the group, with only an empty seat between him and the guitar player with the Devil's Shingle.

"Where's Buck?" One of the musicians asked about the bartender.

"Out back, talking to his liquor distributor." Crankshaft thumbed over his shoulder.

The musicians nodded their acceptance and refilled their beer mugs, before most of them went back to the table in the corner where their instrument cases sat on the floor. They weren't going anywhere until they had gotten paid. Bobby stayed on his bar stool, sipping his drink and looking around as if he had just inherited the joint, before he acknowledged the quiet man in the flat cap a seat away.

"It's Crankshaft, right? Crankshaft—?" Bobby snapped his fingers as he remembered the last name. "Jones, isn't it?"

"Yeah."

"What did you think, Mr. Jones?"

"I think you're going to hell."

"Really? I didn't take you for one of those bible beater types, Mr. Jones."

"I'm not. Fact is, I don't really know what I am, but I'm glad I'm not you. I may not believe in it, but when a man who does is willing to sell his soul, that's pretty low. And when he uses innocent people to do his dirty work for him, then it's even lower." The ace mechanic was even so kind as to lower his voice so the other musicians couldn't hear him as he continued.

"You set Petey Wheatstraw up. Used his own beliefs against him, and even if I don't believe—that's worse than evil. That's just plain mean."

"I didn't mean for Jellyroll to get killed." The damned guitar player couldn't stop smiling.

"I know. That's what's worse. You don't care one way or the other. You almost threw me when you suggested we do something about the murder, but then you were just trying to send the lynch mob after Petey. You weren't even man enough to steal your own trinket. You had to go out and find a handicapped man to do it for you."

"Pretty judgemental, aren't you?" Bobby said.

"Maybe at first— I did think about turning you into the police—but then I thought again. I don't have to judge you, Bobby. You've already sentenced yourself."

Bobby shifted in his seat uncomfortably. "All I did was make a trade for something I wasn't using, anyway."

"What, your brain? The door to hell locks from the inside, Bobby boy. It's already over and you don't even know it."

"So what's it matter to you, if you don't even believe in it?"

"I don't have to believe in it. *You* don't even have to believe in it anymore. The wheels have been set in motion. Your gift is a curse."

Bobby's smile slackened and his eyes narrowed.

"Think about it. Think about what the Devil's Shingle means. Sure you'll be the 'greatest Blues musician on earth.' The public will love you. The money, the women, the liquor and song will all roll in. But this 'gift' comes at a price.

"First, think about what you did to get it, because that's what other people are going to be thinking about. Only they'll be thinking about taking it from you by whatever means necessary. So, if you're lucky, they'll just beat you to death by accident like Jellyroll, instead of coming right out and planning to murder you. It's the death of a thousand cuts. You'll have to spend the rest of your life looking over your shoulder. Because even if I don't believe it, somebody else out there does and it's already too late.

"Even now, you're already smart enough to hide it. But as your popularity soars you're going to have a lot of questions thrown at you. '*Who's going to find out?*' When and Why—lots of Why's! Like '*Why does that person even like me? Do they like me, or is it just the Shingle?*' till you won't even be a person anymore. In the end you'll hate everybody, and the only question you'll have is '*What do you want from me?*' Meanwhile, you'll be questioning your own talent—probably the only part of you that was any good to begin with. No matter what you do, no matter how talented you are, in your own mind the Devil's Shingle will always get the credit."

Crankshaft stood up. He wandered over to Jellyroll's old Resonator guitar in its case on the floor, picked it up and held it at his side as he spoke.

"If you're anything like the others, you'll spend the rest of your life on the road, touring endlessly, working yourself to death due to forces you think are beyond your control. You'll probably be lucky enough to play about three hundred gigs a year—working for the pick—looking over your shoulder and seeing your own death a thousand times a night."

"Then you'll break down—physically, emotionally, anxiously—if you don't work yourself to death first. Or somebody doesn't kill you." Crankshaft smiled and strolled toward the front door with Jellyroll's guitar.

"Hey, that's my guitar!" Bobby said, leaping from his seat.

The rest of the band clambered in front of the door and began to slowly surround the ace mechanic. Hands made fists as the drummer picked up his stool, ready for a fight. Crankshaft didn't bother to turn around as he rolled his eyes at the band and spoke to the cursed man at the bar.

"Not anymore," Crankshaft said and sat the case down on the floor. "It belongs to Petey Wheatstraw, for services rendered." The wiry old soldier finally turned around. Facing Bobby, he moved slowly, glancing warily at the band and scratching at his ribs with his right hand.

But when he extended his hand there was a gun in it.

Crankshaft hadn't spent all his time ignoring his partner. The old dog had a new trick. He stood with his arm extended, a .45 automatic aimed at the guitarist's heart. "Gentlemen, I think we all know that's Jellyroll Hawkins' old guitar," Crank announced to the rest of the band. Still pointing the gun at Bobby, he ratcheted the automatic's hammer back for effect.

Bobby shuddered in his seat.

"That's just one, Robert. And it's still early," Crankshaft said. "You still have to die nine-hundred-and-ninety times more today."

The ace mechanic picked the guitar case up by the handle. No one said a thing. The band parted in front of the door as Crankshaft made his way through. Crankshaft turned in the doorway and smiled before he exited.

"Any of you got problems with me taking the guitar; I suggest you take it up with The First Baptist Church. We wouldn't want Robert Johnson going to hell now, would we?"

As Crankshaft exited and stepped into the early morning haze, for the first time he could ever remember, there was a moment of silence on Maxwell Street.

EPILOGUE

"The most mysterious man in the history of the blues is probably Robert Johnson, a musician who claimed to have sold his soul to the devil in exchange for his talent, and who died violently at an early age— Around 1931 Johnson left the Robinsonville area. Later, his playing had improved to a miraculous degree, leading to extravagant rumors that he had made a 'deal' with Satan.

"Johnson's untimely death came on August 16, 1938, most likely from poisoning by a jealous husband—he was reputed to have a woman in every town."
—The Encyclopedia of Music in the 20th Century

"It may be Robert could have sold himself to the devil. In the way he was, the way he played and acted, he could have felt that he sold his soul. A special feeling could have hit him like he done that and that feeling come out in his music."
—Honeyboy Edwards, Blues Musician

"Johnson sold his soul to play like that."
—Son House, Blues Musician

To this day Robert Johnson is most remembered as the author of "Crossroads Blues," a song where a musician sells his soul to Satan, and the Devil tunes his guitar.

The End

ABOUT OUR CREATORS

Writer

B.C. BELL - is the author and creator of the series TALES OF THE BAGMAN, the story of a 1930s Chicago racketeer turned Robin Hood. Bell has written over a dozen pulp hero adventures, ranging from THE AVENGER to SECRET AGENT X. His book BIPOLAR EXPRESS, the story of a madman trapped in a post-apocalyptic Chicago, made the Horror Writer's Association reading list for 2012. Bell lives with his wife in Chicago and is currently working on a novel-length Weird Tale.

Interior Illustrator

ART COOPER - is a Canadian artist/writer/editor who was a founding partner of Spectrum Publications, which published three bi-monthly fanzines in the early '70's. Art was a member of the inaugural Cartooning program at Sheridan College in Oakville, Ontario, where the guest instructors included such luminaries as Joe Kubert, Neal Adams and Will Eisner. Art contributed to a number of fan publications and penciled two stories for Orb Magazine before getting married and completing his engineering degree. Art has worked as a project manager in the Mining and Metals industry for the past few decades, and has done some freelance advertising work on the side. Art is the proud father of two grown sons, and lives in Mississauga, Ontario with his current wife and daughter.

Cover Painter

SHANE EVANS - lives in small town Whangarei, New Zealand. He has one wife, two boys, two volkswagens and one insane dog. He has been drawing, painting and creating since he can remember. In between the various illustration and airbrushing jobs, he has also been a graphic designer and signwriter. His style and tastes were greatly influenced by the steady diet of b-grade horror films, cult films and macho action movies. The comics that he grew up reading were 2000AD, The Savage Sword of Conan,

Batman, Mad Magazine and others. Some of his favourite artists are Frank Frazetta, Simon Bisley, Dave McKean, John Buscemi and many many more.

You can look at his work online at: www.sevans.co.nz or on deviant art under the name SEVANS73.